"Don't you ⌐ **Indignation** **all but lashir** **reluctantly p** **~~~~~~~~~~ ~~~ image of this woman in his bed.**

"Maybe a little laughter is how we need to deal with this situation. Now please sit down, the poor waitress has no idea if we are staying or going." He tried to instill some order into their meeting, which didn't feel anything like a business lunch.

He liked the way Lydia's brunette hair moved, slipping over her shoulder, the loose curls bouncing with the movement, and the way she tucked it back behind her ears. There was an air of vulnerability about her he didn't buy into at all. There was no way this fiery creature was vulnerable. Spoiled and used to getting her way, yes, but vulnerable, no.

"I'm not entirely sure being forced into a marriage is a laughing matter." She fixed those gorgeous eyes on his face, her full lips pouting slightly, making him briefly wish this was a date and that by the end of the evening he would be able to kiss them. Savagely he pushed those thoughts aside. This was not a time to become distracted.

"Then on that we agree."

Rachael Thomas

——

VALDEZ'S BARTERED BRIDE

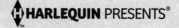

Recycling programs
for this product may
not exist in your area.

ISBN-13: 978-0-373-06114-3

Valdez's Bartered Bride

First North American publication 2017

Copyright © 2017 by Rachael Thomas

Printed in U.S.A.

Rachael Thomas has always loved reading romance, and is thrilled to be a Harlequin author. She lives and works on a farm in Wales—a far cry from the glamour of a Harlequin Presents story—but that makes slipping into her characters' worlds all the more appealing. When she's not writing or working on the farm, she enjoys photography and visiting historical castles and grand houses. Visit her at rachaelthomas.co.uk.

Books by Rachael Thomas

Harlequin Presents

The Sheikh's Last Mistress
New Year at the Boss's Bidding
Craving Her Enemy's Touch
Claimed by the Sheikh
A Deal Before the Altar

The Secret Billionaires

Di Marcello's Secret Son

One Night With Consequences

A Child Claimed by Gold
From One Night to Wife

Brides for Billionaires

Married for the Italian's Heir

The Billionaire's Legacy

To Blackmail a Di Sione

Visit the Author Profile page at Harlequin.com for more titles.

For Marie Dry and the happy memories of the fun time we spent in Madrid and Seville.

PROLOGUE

Middle of September, two months earlier.

'DO YOU REALLY expect me to go through with it?' Raul Valdez's voice thundered around the room, his Spanish words fluid and fast.

'The debt needs to be repaid and, whether you like it or not, the contract your father made before his death with Henry Carter-Wilson still stands. As a member of the board I insist upon it.' Carlos's voice ripped through Raul, increasing his anger to an explosive level.

Raul swore savagely as he glared at the older man. 'Come on, Carlos, we go back further than that.'

'As a long-standing family friend, I urge you to stop looking for someone who doesn't want to be found and marry the girl—as your father obviously intended.'

'Marry her?' Raul couldn't believe he was hearing this, from Carlos of all people.

'Repay the debt, then file for a divorce once the two years are up.'

Rage charged through Raul like a bull. How could his father have done this? But that wasn't a question he needed to ask. He'd never been able to gain his father's approval, had tried all his life to no avail. This was just one more stab at the son he'd never wanted.

'You make it sound so easy.' Raul drew in a deep breath and marched to the windows looking out over Madrid, basking in the late summer sunshine. On paper it did look easy, but marriage was the one thing he'd never wanted.

'It is,' Carlos replied, his tone neutral and matter-of-fact. 'Two years living with a woman who, you've got to admit, is very beautiful, then you can file for a divorce.'

'I have no intentions of marrying anyone. Ever.' Raul strode across the office, the constraint of the walls making him feel more like a caged animal, trapped against its will. Anger at what his father had done mixed with the fear of being controlled by him still becoming a potent cocktail.

Raul stopped pacing and looked out over Madrid again, trying to control his temper. He stayed like that for several minutes, his back resolutely turned to Carlos Cardozo, the man who had been there for him more than his father ever had. *His* father. That was a joke.

He'd always known he'd been a disappointment to

his father, but never had he expected such revelations after his sudden death. He'd never suspected his father had hated him, but then he'd never suspected his father had had another family—another son.

'The only other option you have is to find your half-brother.' Carlos's calm voice brought him out of his dark thoughts and back to the present with a sharp jab of shock. 'Which would mean sharing your inheritance—everything you have built this banking enterprise up to be.'

Raul whirled round. This had been a detail his father's lawyer had revealed, one he'd kept secret since that day. How did Carlos know? 'You know about him?'

'Yes.' Carlos looked him in the eye, challenging him to ask more.

'How long?' Raul took the challenge.

'Long enough to know how this is affecting you now.' Carlos's voice softened a little as he walked over to him.

Raul had been in ignorance of his half-brother's existence until his father's will had been read out two months ago. It seemed Carlos had known the full facts of his father's double life long ago.

'And you didn't think I should know?' His anger rallied again as he glowered at Carlos, the taste of deception filling his mouth with its bitterness.

'I never knew your father would make finding

him a condition to you inheriting. Or that he would attach such a huge financial incentive to that task.'

Huge financial incentive.

That was an understatement.

'That or marry a woman I barely know.' Raul glowered at Carlos, suspicion rising at just how much this man knew.

'Marriage would be the easier option.'

'Is that so?' Raul seriously doubted that. Besides, his brother was out there somewhere.

'It is. You are your father's son. Marriage will be easy for you. Far better than to share all you've worked for.'

Raul turned away again. His world had been tipped upside down and then inside out. In order to inherit the financial company he'd built into a world player, he had to clear one very large debt by either marrying the debtor's daughter, or by acknowledging his half-brother and bringing him into the business as an equal, which would unlock funds that would clear the debt and keep the board of directors happy. If the debt wasn't settled, the company would be sold to the highest bidder.

The fact that his father had even kept those funds hidden exposed the depths of calculation he had gone to, but that he was prepared to risk his company if the debt wasn't settled, to risk the jobs of all the people who worked for Banco de Torrez, was a step too far. What the hell had he been doing loaning that kind of money and why was Carlos the only one privy to such information?

'I could have told you my father would be so calculating, so manipulative—had I known about his *other life*.' Raul found himself snarling those last two words, hating the anger that sliced through him with the sharpest of blades.

'He's your father—doesn't that count for something?' Carlos reached for him; the false show of sympathy and understanding in that gesture was too much. Raul moved away. This man was not the friend he'd always thought—not to him anyway.

'I'm done with my father, so much so that I don't give a damn about inheriting his company. I have built my own as well as expanded his. I don't need this.' Raul marched towards the door. As far as he was concerned the discussion was over; there was nothing more to say.

'What about your mother?' Carlos's next words halted his steps, kept him from walking out for good.

Raul remained with his back to Carlos, breathing deep and slow, clenching his fingers into tight fists at his sides. His mother was the only reason he'd spent the last two months trying to find his half-brother, not wanting the press—or anyone else—to get to her first with the revelation of her husband's secret life. It would finish her.

'You can't walk away, can you, Raul? You can't risk her finding out by reading salacious gossip in the press?' Carlos challenged. Again. Damn him. The man knew just how to twist the situation, how to manipulate him.

Raul whirled round to face Carlos again. 'No, I damn well can't. If not for my mother's happiness, then for all the jobs which depend on me settling this debt by either finding my half-brother or marrying a spoilt little rich girl. Either way I despise my father for it.'

'So why not take the easy option and marry this Lydia girl?'

'That will never happen,' Raul spat officiously at him. After the example he'd seen of marriage, he would rather welcome a stranger into his life, into his father's company. Hell, as far as he was concerned, his brother could have it all if it kept people in work and his mother in ignorance of his father's past actions. He didn't need any of it.

'The board are getting nervous, Raul. They think you've lost your influence, especially after the Lopez deal fell through.' Carlos touched yet another raw nerve, ratcheting up the desire to prove him and every damn member of the board wrong. One lost deal didn't spell the end.

'I haven't given up on that yet, just as I haven't given up on the search for my half-brother.' Raul glared angrily at Carlos, resenting the challenge the man was issuing, inadvertently or not.

'Either way, the debt needs to be settled before the end of the year. Sooner if possible.'

'That's just over three months away. I'll find my half-brother before then, settle the damn debt and keep the scandal from my mother.'

'If you don't, you will have to meet Lydia Carter-Wilson.' Carlos spoke carefully. Quietly.

'If she is anything like she was ten years ago, I would rather lose my father's business.' Raul baulked at the memory of the simpering sixteen-year-old girl on the verge of womanhood who'd looked at him like an adoring puppy. Was that when his father had started loaning funds to hers?

'What about all those people who will lose jobs? Shutting down companies isn't who you are, Raul. Saving them and building them up, giving the people who work within them, a secure life. That's who you are and I've never known you to refuse a challenge yet.' Carlos spoke the truth, but Raul was too angry to acknowledge it right now.

'I need more time.'

'If you haven't found your half-brother by the end of November, I will expect you to announce your engagement to Lydia Carter-Wilson.'

'What if the lady is unwilling?'

Carlos laughed, defusing the tension somewhat. 'You will find a way, Raul. Your charm with the ladies has never failed you yet.'

CHAPTER ONE

Late November

LYDIA MENTALLY BRACED HERSELF for battle, because this was one fight she was not prepared to lose. Over the twenty-six years of her life, she'd perfected the art of hiding her emotions and now she intended to use it fully. Raul Pérez Valdez wouldn't know what had hit him. Ten years ago he'd made her feel totally insignificant, like nothing more than a spoilt little rich girl, and she hated him for that. Ever since she'd gone to live with her grandmother as a child, she'd worked hard to shake off that label.

Any moment he would arrive and walk through the diners of one of London's top restaurants to the intimate candlelit table he'd arranged, referring to it as neutral territory in his blunt email. The mood she was now in, he was going to need every bit of help he could get from the chosen venue, which was anything but neutral if his reputation of romancing women was true. It was very much a setting he would be at home in, whereas she was distinctly uncomfortable in such surroundings, having avoided anything remotely romantic after witnessing so many relationships turn sour, including her own supposed happy ever after.

Irritation filled her as the minutes ticked by. He was late. The time he'd appointed had already passed. Was the man intending to make her suffer even more? Make her so nervous she could easily jump at her own shadow? Or had he decided against the ludicrous deal his father had concocted with hers? Did this mean she was free to go back to her life and not honour the conditions of that deal she'd unwittingly been dragged into? Her father had reached an all-time low with that deal, leaving her to pay the price.

Except she'd had enough. She didn't owe her father anything, not after all the years of ignoring her, unless it suited his latest negotiations, of course. Like the time she'd been paraded as a sixteen-year-old in front of the man she was about to meet, as if she was some sort of bait. That plan had failed—or so she'd thought.

With a huff of irritation, Lydia picked up her purse from the small round table and stood up to leave. She wasn't wasting any more time waiting for Raul Valdez. If he wanted her father's debt settled, he could chase around London after her.

'Going somewhere?' The sultry accent snared her

senses and she turned and looked up into the face of a man so handsome he couldn't possibly be the perpetrator of such dire circumstances. He'd changed, but from the intent look in his inky black eyes she knew without a doubt this was Raul Pérez Valdez, CEO of the Spanish investment bank her father had defaulted to in the most spectacular way.

Every sculpted angle of his face, from the high cheekbones to the Romanesque nose and the deepset eyes, sent her body's senses spinning into overdrive. Memories of being an impressionable girl on the brink of womanhood collided with that reaction and she was unable to quell the erratic racing of her pulse, or the shiver of something she quickly dismissed as nothing more than attraction.

'We had a meeting ten minutes ago.' Her sharp words did nothing to this specimen of cool reserve. The heavy brows lifted slightly in disbelief—or was it amusement? She couldn't tell. The intensity in his eyes increased, but she was determined he wouldn't use his well-known charm on her. She glared at him, hoping the icy coldness she was renowned for showed in all its glory. She wasn't an impressionable sixteen-year-old any more.

'For my lateness, I apologise.' He held the back of the chair she'd just vacated, the expression on his face showing he expected her to sit back down.

Lydia tried to remain focused as she looked up at him, hating the way excitement sparked inside her as his dark eyes travelled down her body, making her display of cold demeanour extremely difficult. She stood boldly as his gaze seemed to rip the black fitted skirt and businesslike white blouse from her. Each second that ticked by increased her vulnerability, raising it higher than it had ever been, and the urge to fight back kicked in. If he was going to blatantly inspect her, she'd return the compliment.

With huge effort she dragged her gaze from the black depths of his eyes, taking in the clean-shaven face, then to the strong neck encased in a pristine white shirt collar, intensifying the olive tones of his skin. His hair was thick and as dark as coal and his broad shoulders gave her the impression they were strong enough to carry any problems. His arms flexed tantalisingly beneath the fine cloth of his suit as he stood and leant slightly on the back of the chair, his cold stare barely masking his irritation.

How would it feel to be held within the strength of those arms? Her pulse leapt at the thought and she fought hard again to quell the instant attraction that had stirred the woman in her she'd long since hidden away. This was not the time to indulge in silly romantic notions and most definitely not with this man, one who'd made his thoughts of her plain many years ago.

'If this meeting was as important as you led me to believe, you would not have been late, Mr Valdez.' Her anger at the way her body had reacted as she'd taken in every detail of this man, and the thoughts that had raced through her mind at the idea of being held in those strong arms, made her voice crisp and sharp.

That impressive control didn't waver.

'You and I are in a position which I am certain neither of us want, Miss Carter-Wilson, and, as I have the solution, I suggest you sit down.' She saw his jaw flex as he clenched his teeth, the only sign she was challenging his outward display of patience.

'The position we are in? You mean the bizarre conditions your father attached to the contract he forced my father to sign?' That sensation of helplessness she'd been fighting for several weeks surfaced again and her voice rose rapidly with each word.

'Exactly that.' The calmness of his voice, together with the silky rich accent, jarred her senses, increasing her wildly overactive anxieties.

'There is no way it can be enforced.' She knew she was beginning to babble, the panic of everything almost too much, and she bit back further words. He had to think she was calm and in control, had to think he'd met his match. His equal.

'If you sit down we can discuss this rationally.' He gestured to the chair, his brow rising in question— or was it amusement?

Unable to keep a sigh of discontent from escaping, she sat down. The need to be in charge, to control the situation she was virtually drowning in, forced her to speak again before he'd sat opposite her at the small and inappropriately intimate table, complete with a red rose and candle.

'I think you need to explain just what kind of business contract your father tricked mine into signing. It is inconceivable that in the twenty-first century two people can be forced to marry because of such devious tactics.' She took a deep shuddering breath, hardly able to comprehend that this nightmare was actually happening.

'That is why I'm here—'

Lydia cut across him, angry at the stupidity of her father for signing a contract with such dire conditions and, even more so, at this cool specimen of male splendour for being so calm and pragmatic about it. 'Mr Valdez, I don't care what is in the contract. I'm not going to marry you. Not ever.'

His dark brows rose and she thought she saw a hint of a smile on his lips. Even worse, his reaction sent a skitter of something she'd never experienced hurtling through her and her pulse leapt just from having that sexy hint of a smile, which had sparked briefly in his eyes, directed at her.

'At least we agree on that.' He sat back in his chair, his dark eyes locking with hers, full of challenge. 'You may be assured I have absolutely no desire to make a spoilt little rich girl my wife.'

So his opinion of her hadn't changed. 'I am no such thing.'

She fought hard to resist the urge to jump up and walk away; only the fact that her solicitor had told her the terms of the contract her father had signed with Banco de Torrez, however bizarre, would stand up in court, kept her from doing just that—for now.

'What about all the properties? Many of them are worth millions. Your father hid them by putting them in your name as he defaulted month after month on the agreement he'd signed with my father.' He folded his arms across his chest, serving only to emphasise the strength in them as the dark grey suit pulled over his biceps. Since when did she ever notice such things about a man?

'That is something I had no knowledge of, but, if they are in my name and worth that much, I will sell them to clear the debt.' The discovery several weeks ago of what her father had done had been just another bit of her life falling to pieces. Angry at the man who was supposed to protect her, she'd maintained a stony silence with him, to show him her disappointment and anger that once again he'd risked everything, including this time her future, her happiness.

Raul looked at her and she knew he didn't believe her. The cold lack of interest was too obvious. Was he really as ruthless in business as those reports she'd read on the Internet implied? She had hoped to strike some sort of deal with him. After all, a man who rarely dated the same woman twice was as unlikely to want marriage as she was.

'I would be more than happy to accept such an offer—'

'Good.' She stood up, content that this absurd conversation was over. 'Then you can liaise with my solicitor over the matter.'

'Do you always talk over people?' His question stopped her as she was about to leave for the second time and she looked down at him, stunned into silence, and the elusive sensation of being in control slipped further away with each erratic heartbeat. From the moment he'd arrived and their eyes had met, she'd lost that control.

Raul had never known such self-assured insolence from a woman as beautiful and alluring as the prim and proper Lydia Carter-Wilson. She certainly didn't want to hear what he had to say and wasn't prepared to listen to his suggestion for dealing with the situation they were both now in. A solution he was certain would be acceptable. Yet it was blatantly clear all this fiery beauty cared about was herself. She hadn't changed a bit since he'd met her ten years ago. Granted, she'd become a beautiful and sexy woman, but she wasn't any different. She was still a spoilt little rich girl. Daddy's princess—and a liar.

He pushed down the irrational anger that engulfed him every time he thought of what his father had done. That last meddling dig at the son he'd never wanted threatened to unleash all the bitterness and contempt he'd kept hidden since his father had died five months ago. The devious old man had even known he was terminally ill and changed his will to get at him one last time.

'No, I don't, but then I've never had the dubious pleasure of lunch with a man like you.' The hot retort fired at him and he couldn't help but smile. It was definitely an inconvenience having to extricate himself from such an agreement with this woman, but he'd certainly not expected to find it so entertaining. She was a bundle of hot sparks and defiance. Just the mutinous tilt of her chin and the rapid rise and fall of her breasts as she glared at him fired something deeper than merely lust. Something he had no wish to get tangled in—ever.

She tempted him, daring him with that sexy body that begged to be made love to, and almost all rational thought slipped from his mind. But he was not his father. He would not be drawn by the lure of sex. His playboy reputation was deserved, but only as part of his armour, his defence in order to remain emotionally intact and very single.

'And what would a man like me be?' He taunted her, enjoying the fire of annoyance that flared in those green eyes, reminding him of the fresh leaves of spring on the trees in Retiro Park, in his city of birth, Madrid.

'A man who thinks he only needs to smile at a woman to have her falling at his feet—or into his bed.' The slight nod of her head, the little *so there* gesture, as she finished speaking made laughing at her impossible to resist.

'My bed?'

'Don't you dare laugh at me.' Indignation hurtled out with those words, all but lashing at him, and he reluctantly pushed away the image of this woman in his bed.

'Maybe a little laughter is how we need to deal with this situation. Now, please sit down. The poor waitress has no idea if we are staying or going.' He tried to instil some order into their meeting, which didn't feel anything like a business lunch.

He watched as she turned to look at the waitress who was approaching their table for the second time. He liked the way Lydia's brunette hair moved, slipping over her shoulder, the loose curls bouncing with the movement, and the way she tucked it back behind her ears. There was an air of vulnerability about her he didn't buy into at all. There was no way this fiery creature was vulnerable. Spoilt and used to getting her way, yes, but vulnerable, no.

'I'm not entirely sure being forced into a marriage is a laughing matter.' She fixed those gorgeous eyes on his face, her full lips pouting slightly, making him briefly wish this were a date and that by the end of the evening he would be able to kiss them. Savagely he pushed those thoughts aside. This was not a time to become distracted.

'Then on that we agree.' He beckoned the waitress forward with a subtle move of his hand and watched as Lydia took the menu, appearing to use it as a shield. Against him or the situation? He watched her long lashes lowering as she read and took the opportunity to study her further. Her skin was pale, making it obvious she hadn't spent the summer in one of her Mediterranean properties. The menu shook very slightly in her hands and he wondered if it was possible for such an audacious woman to be nervous. Much more likely to be anger, he decided, anger that was directed firmly at him. Anger was good, because then at least they could sort out this mess their fathers had selfishly created for them.

As she gave her order her voice became soft and gentle, not at all like the hard and sharp tones he'd been treated to so far. How would she sound if they were here as lovers? Would that softness be beguiling him to take her home and to his bed?

Alarmed by the train of his thoughts yet again, he dragged his mind back to the truth of the situation and placed his order. Employing all the charm he'd perfected as his armour, he smiled at the waitress.

'So, how exactly do you propose to deal with this situation?' The softness had gone and the question fired at him with force. Had she meant to use that word? Propose was the last thing he intended to do. He focused his attention back to the woman opposite him, the woman his father had decided would make him a suitable wife simply because of the substantial properties that she owned and her misfortune to have such a reckless and weak father.

He kept his gaze fixed on the pale beauty of her face, watching for any signs of compliance. 'You have considerable property assets and these were the security used by your father. The terms are more than clear, as I have already informed your lawyer.'

'I have said that I am more than happy to sell them in order to raise the funds required.' She cut across him again, stemming the flow of his well-prepared proposition.

'If that were possible, it would be the most sensible option. Unfortunately, my father has used this security as part of his conditions of his will.' The outrageous terms his father had insisted on still infused him with rage as fiercely as the day he'd discovered what his father had done. A final jab at his son, even after his death, to get just what he wanted.

'His will?' The sharp intake of breath left him in no doubt this was not a piece of information she was aware of. 'I'm sorry about your loss. I had no idea.'

'Please don't waste your sympathy on me.' He pushed away memories of his childhood, of never being able to be what his father wanted, never knowing how to please him and having no idea why. At least that mystery had been solved. 'My father and I were not close.'

That was an understatement. He'd lost all respect

for his father over ten years ago when he'd taken his womanising to a new level, having affairs with young models and actresses who craved the lime-light and high life his name and wealth could give them. The fact that everyone expected him to be just as much of a playboy had irritated him at first, until he'd learnt to use that as defence to keep women at an emotional distance.

The beautiful brunette who'd been dragged into the latest battle his father had set regarded him scep-tically, the spell only broken by the arrival of their wine. He smiled at the waitress as he sampled the wine, aware of Lydia's scrutiny with every breath he took. 'Very good, thank you.'

'Yes, I can see any sympathy would be a waste of time.' Her barbed words flew at him and inwardly he baulked at her directness, but refused to let it show. He was more than used to keeping his emo-tions away from the scrutiny of others, used to put-ting on a show of uncaring detachment, and right now that suited him perfectly.

'So, shall we discuss our options?' Before she could once again talk over him or correct him, he launched directly into all that needed to be said. 'I have no wish to marry anyone, least of all you, but the terms of my father's will are very clear. Upon my father's death, our marriage is the only way your father's debt can be repaid—unless you have such a large sum of money saved?'

'Why can't I just sell the properties?' Her eyes widened with disbelief and her hand came to her face, the tip of one finger dragging across her bottom lip in a very distracting way. He watched as the pink-painted nail dug into the plumpness of her lip, wishing he could sample that plumpness against his lips.

Again he urged his mind back to the situation. Perhaps he was more like his father than he'd ever imagined. The thought sickened him. 'Although the properties are in your name, the terms of the transfer your father carried out means you cannot sell them, that they only remain yours until your marriage, at which point they will become your husband's property.'

'What?' She pressed her fingertips against her mouth, as if to stem the shocked flow of words, and her neat brows furrowed into a frown. He wasn't falling for that.

'Hard to believe, but I'm afraid it's true. It's also a fact my father sought to exploit when he made his will, just months before he died. I am not happy to have inherited your father's debt and with it you as my bride.' He recalled his lawyer's face, full of apology, and the words that had proved beyond doubt how much his father must have disliked him.

I tried to persuade him against it, but he was adamant.

'What century are we in?' Her shock had turned to anger and she flung her hands out over the table, palms upwards in exasperation. 'Just what did they think they were doing?'

'It appears we have both been little more than pawns in their game and it's time now to take control, to thwart whatever it was they each intended.'

'At least now we are on the same page. I have no intention of marrying someone who wants me for what I have. I almost travelled that road and I'm not going there again.' Her burst of irritation held a hint of passion, intriguing him in a way he was far from comfortable about.

'Are you holding out for love, Lydia?' It was the first time he'd used her name and it shocked him how he liked to say it as he looked into her beautiful face. If circumstances were different, he'd be tempted to reach out and push her hair back from her face, revealing her beauty. But he couldn't go there. He didn't seek the confines of marriage, so for now it was better to hide behind the mask of a hardened businessman.

Lydia's pulse leapt as he said that word and looked into her eyes. The unyielding blackness of his sent skitters of awareness all over her. Every part of her body was tuned into his, every move he made only intensified it, but the mention of love halted all that, as if she'd just careered into a brick wall.

'I have no intention of wasting my time holding out for love.' She bristled at the memory of the man

she'd thought she'd loved, the man she'd believed
had loved her until she'd discovered he'd also been
in the habit of loving as many other women as he
could. By that point she and Daniel were engaged.
This had rankled her father and, just to show him
she'd make her own decisions in life, she'd accepted
Daniel's apology. Something she deeply regretted. It
would have been almost preferable to have her father
look at her with that *I told you so* expression than
the humiliation after Daniel had left her because she
no longer had anything to offer him, something her
father had made very clear to him, although at that
point she'd not understood exactly what he'd meant.

Now she did. It was the contract her father had
signed with Raul Valdez's father, using her as his
leverage, his security.

'So cynical, Lydia. Are you not in search of your
Mr Right, the man to live happily ever after with?'
His accented voice sent a shiver of awareness over
her and she knew a flush of colour had spread over
her face.

Who was he to mock such dreams? He was a
complete playboy.

'Once bitten, twice shy, as they say.' She couldn't
help the light and flirty tone of her voice and to hide
her embarrassment she took a sip of her wine. 'But
that is not why we are here, to discuss such nonsense
as love, Mr Valdez, is it?'

'No, we are not.' He snapped the words out, his

accent sharp, and she sensed the impatience in him. Or was it irritation? 'We are here because your father defaulted on his loan.'

Before he could say any more Lydia cut across him once more, not missing the frown of annoyance, which gave her a strange sense of satisfaction. 'And because your father saw fit to use that default in the most devious and unethical way.'

'I agree,' he said and leant forward in the seat, his dark eyes penetrating hers, preventing her from doing anything other than looking into them, but they were cold and she shivered slightly. 'That is why we are here. To extricate ourselves from a marriage I certainly don't want and it would seem you share that view.'

'I still don't see why I can't just sign some of the properties over to you, or sell them and clear the debt.' She wished now she'd had a proper meeting with her solicitor instead of the rushed phone call. She hadn't understood all he'd told her and in all honesty she couldn't believe what her father had done.

'You do not own them, Lydia. They are only yours until you marry, at which time they will pass into the legal possession of your husband.'

She recalled an argument with her father almost a year ago, one of those rare meetings of father and daughter. He'd been smugly pleased with his latest plot to manipulate her into marriage for the good of his company. He'd told her he had found her a hus-

band and that this time she would have no choice
but to do as she was told. She'd refused, telling him
she and Daniel were engaged, but that had been no
deterrent to the lows her father had stooped to in
order to save himself from financial ruin. She'd had
no idea his vast property portfolio had been put into
her name until her marriage.

'By that you mean you.' She put down her wine
glass and glared at him, everything clear at last.
'Your father added the marriage clause in his will
to trick my father.'

'I consider it more of a shrewd tactic to safeguard
the considerable amount of money he had loaned to
your father's business. He must have been sure your
father wouldn't obtain such levels of funding through
the usual channels and added the extra condition
in his will, should the debt remain unsettled in the
event of his death.'

'I hardly think forcing either of us into marriage
is shrewd or businesslike. It's medieval.' She stumbled over the words as she realised how futile they
were and when a smile tugged at the corners of his
lips she wished she were bold enough to get up and
walk away.

'After our marriage, all the properties will become
mine and therefore the debt will be repaid and the
board of directors satisfied. The only issue is that we
must remain married for two years—living together.'

'Are you actually suggesting we get married, just

to clear the debt? I thought you were against any such idea as much as I am.' Lydia couldn't take it in. Married. To this man. For two years.

'That depends on how much you want to help your father.'

Lydia didn't have to think very hard on that one. She didn't want to help her father, but she did want to protect his mother, her grandmother. The woman who'd cared for her, loved her as a daughter. She was the only reason she was still here having this discussion.

'Of course I want to help my father, but I will not marry anyone to do that.' She wasn't about to enlighten Raul Valdez to the fact that her father had tried several times to push her into a marriage that would financially benefit him. The fact that this man's father could possibly succeed where hers had failed was not a pleasant prospect.

'In that case you will be interested to hear of my solution.' Her attention was caught not only by his words, but by the tone of his voice.

'Which is?'

'I suggest we make the marriage and clear the debts. We can lead separate lives whilst living in the same place. After two years, I will not contest a divorce.' He sat back in his chair, the expression on his handsome face close to being smug.

'Is that the best you can do?' Irritation surged through her. Had he met her here to put forward a suggestion that was at the moment the only obvious conclusion? She was so angry with her father. He could have warned her of this, months ago. He must have known he couldn't make the repayments. Now she understood why he'd made it so easy for her to keep up her annoyed silence. He'd gone to ground, hiding like a coward. 'Why have you left it five months to contact me? You must have been made aware of the will conditions months ago.'

'I had other, more pressing issues to deal with.'

'Such as?'

He looked at her as if assessing her ability to be trusted and, just as when he'd first swept his gaze over her, the scrutiny did strange things to her. 'I have been trying to contact a family member whose existence I only discovered upon the reading of the will. If found, that person would offer a very different option for both of us and there is a large financial reward which can be used to clear your debts, but I have as yet been unable to find that person.'

'So, in the meantime, you thought you'd come and force me into a two-year marriage.' Irritation rushed through her. They weren't getting anywhere.

'I am still intending to search for that person, but your father has not made any further payments and has managed to evade all attempts at a meeting. I now have no choice. The board is calling for settlement of the debt. They will not wait any longer. Our engagement must be announced.'

He sat back and sipped the last of his wine, the calm and unruffled exterior unsettling her more than she cared to admit. 'There are agencies for such things.' The confusion on his face as she derailed the topic was priceless and for a brief moment she wanted to laugh. 'Finding missing family members, that is.'

'If you wish to make it public, then yes, there are.' He clenched his jaw as he finished speaking.

'You want to find someone yet keep it secret?' That made no sense whatsoever and at the same time intrigued her. Who did this power-hungry man wish to contact and why?

'It is not something I want the press to get hold of.' The annoyed growl of his voice gave her immense satisfaction but as she took a sip of wine an idea filtered through her mind. Genealogy was something she was very interested in and she'd spent long happy hours helping friends trace their family roots back many generations. Was it possible she could provide what this man wanted? Maybe there was a deal to be made here?

'That sensitive, is it?' She toyed with him, like a cat who had stumbled upon a mouse, enjoying the sensation, even if only briefly, of power.

'Yes, as a matter of fact it is, but it bears no relevance to our discussion.' The curt tone of his voice blended with his accent and she wondered what he would sound like if he were whispering words of love. Except a man like him didn't indulge in love—only lust.

'Supposing I was able to find this family member—discreetly, of course.'

'You?' The surprise in his deeply accented voice sent a smile of satisfaction spreading across her lips. He obviously thought she was nothing more than an empty-headed socialite, who did nothing but party and shop.

'Yes, me. It could clear the debt and relieve us of the need to get married.' It was also far more than that for her. She wanted to hold on to all she'd worked for in life and if this man could sweep in and demand the properties her father had put in her name, would he then want all she had? Her business?

'Go on.'

'I happen to have a passion for genealogy.'

'A passion?' His brows rose and a shiver of awareness spread all over her as he said the word, giving it a totally different connotation from the context she'd meant. 'Now you have aroused my interest. But how can it help with this matter?'

Much to her disgust heat rushed to her cheeks and yet again she lifted her chin and fixed him with a piercing glare. She couldn't let it show just how much he was affecting her, how he was making her stomach flip and her heart pound like a lovesick teenager. Not when she'd sworn she'd never indulge in such nonsense. Hadn't her time with Daniel been enough to warn her off?

'I'll make a deal with you, Mr Valdez. If I find this person, all the debts will be cleared without the need for marriage.'

'That's a massive charge for such a service when I could hire an agency, as you say.'

'But would you have the confidentiality you require?' She waited, hardly able to breathe, the anticipation immense. Had she actually managed to dig her way out of the mess her father had landed her in?

'It's still a high price, Miss Carter-Wilson. Are you sure you can deliver?' He leant forward, his forearms on the table, his long tanned fingers holding the stem of the wine glass.

'Yes.' She crossed her fingers beneath the table and smiled boldly at him.

'How long?'

'That depends on many things. Months at least.'

'You don't have months.' The brittleness of his tone made her blink rapidly.

'Weeks, then.'

'Four at the most.' He assessed her again and she wondered if he sensed her panic.

'In that case you have yourself a deal—but be warned, if this is leaked before I am ready, or you are not successful, then I will want full and immediate payment of the debt, which would mean you as my wife.'

'That threat won't be necessary, Mr Valdez.' She kept her voice firm as she put out her hand to shake on the deal. 'I suggest we meet again as soon as possible, then you can give me any information you already have before you return to Spain.'

'If you are investigating my family, I will be keeping a close watch on what you are doing. Which means, Miss Carter-Wilson, *you* will return to Madrid with me.'

CHAPTER TWO

RAUL COULD HARDLY believe the surprising deal he was about to agree on with this woman. He'd been immediately captivated by her beauty, but had pushed that aside, unable to think past the terms of his father's will or the fact that it appeared ever more likely that he was going to have to do the unthinkable and marry.

He had no desire to get married to any woman. Least of all one his father had tricked him into marrying. The last thing he needed right now was the constant temptation that this woman would represent if she came back to Madrid with him. From the moment he'd first seen her, annoyed and angry at his late appearance, he'd been fighting the pull of attraction that insistently demanded satisfaction.

He couldn't act on it, not when it was the one thing his father had wanted, obviously considering him as much of a womaniser as he had been. Did his father recall the time he and Lydia had met? Had she been part of his plans even then? But what was there to gain from two years of marriage? That was the part that didn't yet make sense.

As he'd arrived at the busy London restaurant, decked out for Christmas, the one thing he hadn't anticipated was that Lydia would hold cards of her own—and be more than willing to put them into play.

Had she sensed how much he needed to track down Max? Did she really have the connections to trace people or was family history just the passing fancy of a rich girl with too much time on her hands? He had little option but to trust her now and cursed himself for having confided in her. Her offer of a deal, even one as outrageous as that, was one he wasn't able to refuse. Not now she could walk away and spill the long-kept family secret he'd only recently discovered. There would of course have to be a back-up plan, one that would mean he wasn't about to risk his business reputation now that he'd finally proved he was not the same man as his father to those that mattered in the business world.

Until recently, he'd been unable to work alongside his father and had started buying up small and struggling businesses, turning them around and either selling them on or trading their shares. It was far more than just the banking business his father had operated. It was a way of helping people and now the Lopez deal was back on the table. His biggest yet.

'You want me to come to Madrid? To drop everything at this time of year just so that you can trace a long-lost relative?' Lydia's shock-infused words dragged him back to the hustle and bustle of the busy London restaurant.

'And what keeps you so busy, Lydia? Parties? Shopping? All of that happens in Madrid too.' Annoyance filled each word. He hadn't expected instant compliance from her, but he had anticipated she'd be ready to do anything to avoid her father's debts.

'Don't assume you know me.' Her eyes sparked angrily at him.

'I don't assume anything other than you will come to Madrid, trace the person I am looking for and settle your debt. Unless you wish to be married before Christmas?'

'I will not go to Madrid on your whim.' She pulled back her hand before he could shake on the deal and he had to suppress the urge to smile. He liked the anger that sparked in her eyes brighter than the Christmas lights of London. He liked the way her lips parted in almost total contrast to that anger. What he didn't find so appealing was his questionable urge to kiss those lips until desire replaced the anger in her eyes.

'Then there is only one alternative open to us.' He let his words hang heavily between them and for the briefest of seconds it was only the two of them. The noise of the other diners slipped away and all he could hear was the rhythmic thump of his heart. He couldn't let her walk away now. He had to find Max as discreetly as possible—and quickly.

'Which is?' The brittle words snapped from her and he became aware of everyone around them once more.

She scowled at him, suspicion in those sexy green eyes, and he decided perhaps it wouldn't be so very bad to be bound in marriage to such a fiery beauty. Two years living as her husband would at least be entertaining.

'You or your father must settle the debts—in full. By the end of the year.'

'By the end of the year? That's little over a month away.'

'The debt must be settled, Lydia, by either full payment or marriage.'

'Believe me, Mr Valdez, if I could make the payment I would, but I can't.'

A spark of fury rose in her voice and a smile pulled at his lips. Instantly her mouth pressed into a firm line of annoyance, which only made the urge to smile at her greater.

'Then you have no alternative but to come back to Madrid and either find the person I am looking for, quickly and discreetly, or announce our engagement. The terms of my father's will state there is a financial reward for finding that person. Enough to cover the debt.'

She shook her head in denial, her soft dark hair

bouncing invitingly on her shoulders, snagging his
attention all too easily. 'No, I won't leave London
now. I can't.'

'A lover?'

'Not that it's any of your business, but no.'

'Then you will become my wife and settle your
father's debts—unless your claim is true.'

He wouldn't enlighten her yet to the fact that they
would have to be seen as a couple, seen to be preparing for their nuptials. Carlos had insisted that would
be the only way to satisfy the board of directors that
he was calling in the debt, that his bride was willing.

'If I am not about to waltz off to Madrid with
you, I am hardly likely to agree to a marriage, whatever the conditions attached to the deal my father
signed.'

He watched as her eyes narrowed with anger and
her lips pressed together and as much as he wanted to
kiss those lips until they softened he knew he never
could. That would be indulging a side of him he had
no wish to explore, be it playboy or something more
emotionally involved.

However, her father's debt was to be settled, she
was well and truly off-limits and he certainly didn't
need the complication of having to resist an ill-timed
attraction. He needed the board off his back, to know
the debt would be settled. Then he could resume his
search for Max, which now seemed much more hope-
ful if Lydia Carter-Wilson did really have a passion

for family history. But what would she make of his family, of the tangled web of deceit that had corrupted recent generations?

More to the point, could he trust her? If this got out it could undo all the good work he'd done to prove to the business world he was a man of morals and high values. A man to be trusted.

'I can of course call in the debt right now.' He could almost feel the angry vibe coming across the table at him and wondered what her reaction would be if they hadn't been having this conversation in such a public place. Would she have given vent to her anger or would she have been as controlled as he was?

'You wouldn't dare.' The whispered words had a hiss of anger in them and his body responded wickedly, the earlier urges to kiss her returned in full force. Only the desire to be different from his father had made him accept the somewhat desperate bargain Lydia had made. It would be a high price, but one worth paying if it avoided the messy tangle of marriage.

'Don't underestimate me, Lydia.' He knew he sounded hard, more of a snarl, but he had to instil such aggression. He needed to make this deal, because he had never expected to be filled with lustful need for the woman he might well have to make his temporary wife.

'It is you who underestimates me, Mr Valdez.'

Despite the anger that still simmered in her eyes he detected a hint of compliance in her voice.

'I never underestimate anyone I do business with and you are certainly no different.' He wouldn't tell her that he'd done his homework on her, found out all he needed to know about the woman who could become his wife. 'Whatever deal we strike, it is for business and nothing more.'

'Nothing at all?'

'No, nothing. It will be a marriage in name only and will end in exactly two years.'

'Before I commit myself, I think you had better tell me exactly who it is I am locating for you.' The frivolous tone of her voice belied the inner turmoil he could see playing out in those expressive eyes. He doubted she could hide anything from him and he certainly hadn't missed that spark of attraction that had briefly showed through all the irritation he'd witnessed in their depths. Her pretty face was so expressive he could read every emotion that crossed it, including the attraction that had sprung as instantly to life as when they'd first met.

Whatever it was sizzling between them, she was as aware of it as he was.

'I am not sure I can trust you yet.' He veered towards caution. She could take the secret he'd uncovered, which would blow his family wide open, and sell it to the press for a huge amount. Maybe not enough to clear her father's debts, but it would still damage his business and his father's, which was precariously positioned with share prices falling since his sudden death. He would not allow it to happen—whatever the cost. He was more than prepared to sacrifice his bachelor status—temporarily—to calm the nerves of the board.

'Then you have wasted my time and yours.' The crispness of each word jarred his senses and he quickly tried to rationalise the situation.

With one call to the press she could destroy his family and his business, but it would ultimately drag her father into the limelight. She appeared to have as little desire for an arranged marriage as he did and even professed to have the skills and knowledge he needed to trace his half-brother. But would she be discreet?

His father had been manipulative to the end. If Lydia successfully found Max, the half-brother he'd never known anything about, then he could claim the money, clear her debts and release them both from the need to marry. His father had excelled himself this time, but had his plan been to force him to marry or bring his unknown half-brother into the business?

'Your father has a debt to pay, Lydia, and I am collecting it—from you. If you can indeed trace the person I am looking for, make contact without arousing the suspicion or interest of the media, then your father's debt will be cleared immediately. Marriage in any form will not be necessary.'

'If you are so against the idea of marriage too, why don't you just pay it off now?' That was exactly the question he'd put to Carlos and his legal team and even now he could feel the cold fear sink through him as he recalled Carlos's reply.

'Such an action will invalidate the will and your father's business will no longer be yours. Failure of any kind to clear the debt will result in the business being sold.'

He had to convince Lydia. There was no way he was letting anyone get his hands on a company he'd painstakingly expanded. 'When I find the person I am looking for it unlocks funds, more than enough to clear your father's debts.'

'So this is all about money? Silly me, I thought you had sentimental reasons for wanting to find this person.' The accusation in her eyes was clear, but she could think what she liked. He'd never have to see her again after this.

'Yes, it's about money—as all business is.'

'So, who is this person? Is it a love child you abandoned and now want to bring out into the open?'

Such an accusation made it clear she'd researched him too and believed him to be as much of a playboy as his father had been. Maybe that was for the best. She didn't seem the type to enter into brief affairs merely to satisfy a sexual attraction. This was a woman who would demand so much more from a lover, whatever her earlier protestations had been.

'It is a love child, yes.' He flaunted the truth before her, aware of the conclusions she was making.

'I hate men like you.' She snapped the words at him and he smiled lazily. He hadn't fathered any children. That was something he'd been extremely careful of, but he enjoyed seeing the anger mix with contempt, filling her eyes, again letting him know exactly what she was thinking.

'Not as much as I dislike women who jump to conclusions.' He sat and watched the questions race across her face. 'It is not my child.'

'So if it's not your love child, whose is it?' Her fine brows rose elegantly in question and the satisfaction that danced in her eyes told him she thought he was lying.

'As I have said, it is not mine.' He wasn't ready to give her the secret that had stayed hidden for so many years. All the times he'd tried to be the son his father had wanted had been in vain and now, with the discovery of Max, his half-brother, it had all become perfectly clear why.

'You are going to have to tell me, if I am to trace this person.' A haughty note had entered her voice. She thought she'd got him on the run, thought she now held the power. Never. But he'd allow her to think that. For a while at least.

'It is my father's son I wish to find.'

Lydia's stomach plummeted. She'd been challenging him, pushing him to reveal his true self to her, and it had just backfired spectacularly. The fierce expression on his face warned her she'd gone too far, pushed too hard. Would he now revoke the offer, force her to find an extortionate amount of money to settle her father's debt? Or worse, marry him?

Suddenly she was that awkward sixteen-year-old again being introduced to Raul by her father. She'd smiled at him, pleased to know that someone closer to her own age would be at the dinner party her father had insisted she attend with him, but Raul had looked down at her with barely concealed lack of interest.

Not that that had stopped the heady attraction she'd instantly had for him and she'd been glad she'd chosen the fitted black dress that had made her feel taller, more attractive and much more grown up. Stupidly, she'd hung on every word Raul had said as they'd been placed next to one another at the dinner table. She'd liked him—more than liked him—and had wanted him to notice her, to like her too. She'd wanted to be more than friends and had already wanted him to be the one she experienced her first kiss with.

All evening she'd tried everything to get his attention, even trying to use her classroom Spanish.

'If you can't say it correctly, don't bother.' The high and mighty put-down had done just that, crashing all the dreams of a friendship, or more, with him.

'I don't have much call to use the language,' she'd

retorted, her cheeks flaming with embarrassment. How had she thought him nice? How had she even begun to imagine that he might like her, might want to be friends, go on a date?

'Then I suggest you stick to your usual shopping and partying and give languages a miss.'

'But I'm going to study languages at university,' she'd replied with a gauche smile.

He'd looked at her then, his dark eyes locking with hers, and she'd held her breath, wondering if he was teasing her—teasing her because he liked her.

'Don't. You clearly don't have any talent for Spanish, exactly what I'd expect from Daddy's little princess who does nothing other than look pretty.' The scathing tone of his voice as his gaze had travelled down her had left her in no doubt that he didn't like her, that he despised her and all he thought she was.

She'd bit back a temper-fuelled retort and vowed that one day, she'd tell him exactly what she thought of him and she'd do it fluently in his language. If he thought she was a spoilt little thing, that was fine by her, but her sense of injustice didn't leave her, not even when she and her father left the dinner party. It had stayed with her, adding to all the insecurities her father had instilled in her.

Now she looked at Raul, ten years older, anger at what her father had done mixed with sympathy for this proud man. Her father's deception, the way he'd forced her mother to leave with his detached and cold ways, his constant need to make the next million before losing it again, seemed minor compared to the family secret Raul had just revealed.

'I'm sorry, I had no idea.' Her voice softened, but it did nothing to the feral expression on Raul's face. He was a man who didn't show softer emotions, that much was clear.

'I have only just discovered the existence of my half-brother. He and I are due to inherit from my father's estate.'

'I don't understand.' She was perplexed by the unveiling of the last few minutes. 'Your father must have known about him, to have included such conditions in the will.'

'He knew. He also knew that I wouldn't want to marry anyone, least of all the daughter of one of his debtors.'

'We have both been set up.' Shock set in and the full implications of the situation she was in finally hit home. How could her father have been so cruel? How could he have used her like this? She could almost imagine him concocting this strange deal with Raul's father. Two heartless men together.

'It would appear so. My father knows that money will motivate me over marriage.'

She tried not to feel insulted, tried not to feel glad that there was a way out of this mess and once she was out of it she'd insist her father sold the properties to repay the debt that, as far as she was concerned, he would still have to Raul. Debts had to be honoured.

'I need to find my brother, preferably without any media attention. I have no wish for the circus they can create or to expose my father's weakness, which will push the company further into the wrong kind of spotlight, not to mention destroy my mother.' His eyes were harder than ever, like a heavy thundercloud about to unleash its fury. Did he hate the brother he'd never met?

Questions raced through her mind, but one had to be asked. 'So why trust me, someone you barely know, with such sensitive information?'

'Because you're as against the idea of marriage as I am and claim to have what I need. Added to that, you are your father's only hope of clearing his debt without dragging his long-standing family name through the bankruptcy courts. That in itself should ensure your compliance with my request.'

He was right about that. If there had been another way to settle this she wouldn't have even met with him today. Her relationship with her father was strained to say the least, but she didn't want the family's name brought into disrepute. Her grandmother might be elderly, but it would break her heart and after what her mother and father had done to her with their selfish actions she would never do anything to upset the only person in the world who had shown her genuine love and affection.

'And there is no other way?'

He paused for a moment and, although those dark eyes were focused on her, she was sure his thoughts were far away. A pang of sympathy zipped through her for him. How would she feel if she suddenly discovered that she had a half-brother or sister?

'I either find my half-brother or we must marry.' His accented voice was sharp as he set out the alternative and totally obliterated that misguided sympathy.

At least any marriage that did have to be made would be purely for the purpose of transferring her property assets to settle the debt. The fact that he wouldn't contest a divorce went some way to settling the unease that still ran through her. He obviously didn't have any intention of making her truly his wife.

So why did disappointment filter through her? Surely she had got over that teenage crush? He might be handsome and possess a lethal charm, if the waitress's reaction to him was anything to go by, but succumbing to his looks and charm was unthinkable. She would never give him the satisfaction.

As if to prove the point, their meals arrived and that skilful charm once again melted the waitress into a puddle. Lydia shook her head in disbelief and looked down at the food she suddenly had no appetite for.

'I don't need to go to Madrid with you. I can work from here.' She had her own business to run and in the final weeks before Christmas it would be busy. Added to that the idea of going to Madrid with this man was not one she welcomed, but the prospect of marriage, even if it was only on paper, was infinitely more unappealing.

'Your enthusiasm for my company warms me.' He mocked, but there was a hint of a mischievous smile on his lips, which she couldn't help but respond to. 'But you will come to Madrid. That is non-negotiable.'

Raul watched the battle play out in those expressive eyes. He could see every twist and turn of her doubt and reluctance, mirroring all he'd felt when he'd realised just what his father had done.

'Neither of us have much choice in this arrangement.' He tried to avoid becoming sidetracked by her long lashes as they lowered over her eyes, shielding his view into her soul. He hadn't expected to find a solution to the problem of tracing his half-brother when he'd made arrangements to meet her, just as he hadn't expected to find the spark of desire from the very first moment he'd seen her, anger sparking from her as she prepared to leave.

'Before I go anywhere with you, or make any kind of formal agreement, I will need a written contract, Mr Valdez. I need it in writing that if I find your brother, my father's debts will be settled.' She hesitated. 'And if the worst happens and we have to marry, it will be nothing more than a deal on paper.'

So she didn't trust him either. He admired her courage to sit there and demand a contract for the repayment of her father's debt. 'I will have it drawn up and you can sign it as soon as we arrive in Madrid.'

He'd already decided they would leave tomorrow as he had no intention of giving her too much time to begin enquiries into the whereabouts of his half-brother, Max. He might not yet have given her any details, but he couldn't risk her discovering the full extent of his father's treachery, not until he could be sure she wouldn't leak the story to the press. He had no intention of putting his mother, the only person to have shown him genuine love, through such a public humiliation.

His father had treated him and his mother badly. For eight years he'd led a double life, deceiving not only his wife and son, but another woman and child. Raul remembered the day his mother had found out about his affair. He could still hear the hurt echoing from the past as she'd told his father the marriage was over, that he could do what he liked but she and her son were staying where they belonged. That was the start of the coldest example of marriage he'd ever seen. What if he too was destined for the same?

Now that he'd discovered his father had turned

his back on a child and its mother, Raul wanted to deal with it. He'd grown up with a father in his life and another child hadn't. It didn't sit well and he was determined to do all he could to make some kind of amends for the past. He only wished his father were here to listen to the tirade of angry words he had for him. Given his father's reputation, it was worryingly possible that more children had suffered the same fate.

He sat back and pressed his fingers together in a steeple, forcing all the hurt and rejection from his childhood down, trying hard to keep those negative emotions out of play. Now was not the time to relive that constant feeling that he'd never be good enough for his father, no matter what he did.

He had two choices. To ignore his half-brother and marry Lydia to settle a debt or take Lydia's offer, find Max and hopefully free them of need to marry. He didn't have to think too long about that answer. His father might have wished Max away by ignoring him, but he didn't want to do that—just as much as he didn't want to enter into the negative binds of marriage. If his father thought the threat of sharing his inheritance would be enough to force him into marriage, he had miscalculated—badly.

'What if I don't find your brother?' The question slipped innocuously from her lips and he looked at them, briefly wondering how they'd taste and feel beneath his.

He bit down on such traitorous thoughts, focusing instead on the shock of all he'd discovered yet had been unable to uncover himself. 'Half-brother.'

'Half-brother, brother...what difference does it make? What if I don't find him?'

'It makes a great deal of difference, Lydia. You too are an only child. How would you feel if you'd just discovered you had a sibling?'

'That's not what we are discussing,' she fired hotly back at him.

'If you don't find my half-brother within four weeks, then you will become my wife and your father's debts will be cleared.'

'For two years.' The dejection in that statement almost got to him. Almost.

He nodded. '*Sí*. After which you can file for divorce.'

'Four weeks is not very long to undertake such a task,' she said as she took a sip of her wine, the action once again drawing his attention to her lips, causing his mind to wander in directions it shouldn't be going in. 'And it will be Christmas too.'

'All the more reason to succeed. Four weeks is all you have. If you fail, Lydia, you will become my wife on Christmas Eve.'

CHAPTER THREE

MADRID WAS THE last place Lydia had expected to find herself and Raul's overpowering presence made it seem even more unreal, as if she were in the middle of a dream—or a nightmare.

The flight to Spain on his private jet had been difficult and with just the two of them she'd wondered what they were going to talk about. Thankfully he'd used the time to read over some paperwork and she'd given the outward appearance of relaxing even though inside she'd been a jumbled mess of questions. Now however, as they travelled in the back of his chauffeur-driven car through the bustle of the city's streets, lit up with festive cheer even in the late afternoon, she couldn't escape the fact that his full attention was focused on her.

'How long do you anticipate it will take to find my brother?' It was the first time he'd referred to him not as his half-brother and she wondered why, when he was notorious for being a playboy himself, he had been so affronted by the discovery of another sibling. But then she knew better than most that families could portray a façade of happiness when underneath secrets and lies were hidden away. It was an art she too had now perfected.

'I have no idea, not until you can give me some more information, but don't forget this is not my profession. Researching family history is just an interest of mine. I'm not claiming to be an expert.' She didn't like the way his eyes narrowed, a sign she'd quickly realised was one of irritation. Neither did she like the rush of panic that swept over her. What if she failed?

You can't fail, so you're not going to.

'What *is* your profession?' The glacial tone of his voice held scorn and she had to fight hard against the urge to smile smugly at him because one thing was certain and that was the fact that he still labelled her a spoilt little rich girl—Daddy's heiress who didn't know how to do anything other than party and shop.

'My profession?'

'Yes, what is it that you do each day?'

Would he be surprised if she told him that she'd graduated from university with an honours in Spanish? What about if she told him she'd taken her love of fashion and now had two very successful luxury boutiques? One in London and one in Paris. She'd never linked them to her family name, wanting only to succeed on her own merit. And she had. Briefly she wanted to shock him with that piece of information, but what right did he have to know everything about her? All she needed to do was trace his brother and it could be done in a matter of a week or two—if she was lucky.

'I think it's fair to say my strengths lie in the retail market.' She teased around the truth, played on what he still thought of her and couldn't help but smile as he scowled at her. Let him think what he wanted to. Far better that he thought she spent money rather than earned it. After all she was here in Madrid to settle her father's debts, so that she could move on and put the shambles that was her childhood behind her. She had only ever been an inconvenience to her mother, who now barely contacted her, and her father had always been a shadowy figure in the background of her life. It had been her grandmother who'd brought her up.

'You will of course find plenty of opportunity for such retail strengths here in Madrid.' The icy tone of his voice was almost enough to make the sun race behind the gathering rain clouds. If he tried hard enough he might even make it snow. She smiled at the thought as she watched him, his handsome face full of undisguised annoyance. 'Especially at this time of the year.'

'Yes, but there are of course more important matters than shopping right now—like which hotel do you suggest I stay at?' She hadn't been away from home for some time and was looking forward to the luxury of time out, satisfied that her recently appointed London manager would handle almost any problem that should arise. Not that she intended to stay for an extended length of time. Once she'd handed over the information Raul Valdez had requested, she'd leave, free of debt and free of obligation—to anyone. Even if it took two weeks she'd still be back in London before Christmas.

'You will be staying with me.' His words dropped into the ocean of her thoughts, shattering them as the waves of implications spread outwards.

'With you?' She looked across the car at him, suddenly feeling trapped. There was no way she could stay with him, not when he unleashed the kind of reaction that made her doubt her ability to ignore his presence or the sizzle of attraction that rampaged through her just from one look of those sexy dark eyes. She didn't need or want the complications of a man in her life. Daniel had killed those silly dreams even if her parents' hostile marriage hadn't.

She looked away from those brooding eyes and the sensation that he could read every thought that ran through her mind. Instead she focused on the passing city streets. What was the matter with her? Since when did she go all gooey over a man? She'd never been like this before.

'I have a perfectly adequate guest suite in my apartment.' A smile teased around his lips as she looked back at him, instantly wishing she hadn't as a zip of something she really didn't want to acknowledge charged through her.

'I thought you wanted to keep your search quiet and away from the press. What if they see you and I together and come up with the wrong answer?' She scrabbled for a reason not to stay with him.

'If that does happen, our *romance* will be much more of interest than the research you will be doing.' The heavy line of his brows lifted and this time he did smile. One of satisfaction and she swallowed down against the flutter that rose swiftly from her stomach, making her head light. She wasn't a teenager being chatted up by the hottest guy she'd ever met. She was a grown woman who knew her own mind, one who would make him regret ever looking at her with such disdain.

'Our romance?' A nervous laugh escaped with those words, intensifying her anger at the situation she was in.

'The perfect cover for your investigation, no?' The car stopped and he looked at her, the flirtatious mood of seconds ago disappearing. 'Do not forget who has the debt to settle, Lydia. You are not in a position to make demands or question my decisions and we will act as if we are in a relationship, as if we both accept the terms of the contract your father signed with mine.'

Before she could hurl any retort at him, he got out of the car and seconds later her door was opened by his driver, making exactly what she wanted to say difficult, if not impossible. She had made the original bargain, striking a deal that would help her, and he had turned it around to suit his needs.

He spoke in a flourish of Spanish to the driver; the sexy undertones of his voice in a language she loved knocked her thoughts off balance. But that little nugget of information was one she'd keep to herself—for now. As the satisfaction of that thought settled over her, he turned to her and spoke softly in English, putting his hand gently in the small of her back. 'This way, *querida*.'

The sensation of his hand, barely touching her, stifled any kind of reaction and like a meek lamb she did his bidding, glancing up quickly at the old but ornate building they were entering. The sound of the almost constant flow of traffic was snuffed out as the doors closed behind them.

'I'm still not sure it is right that I stay with you. I could easily find a hotel near here and still be able to do the research.' She tried one last time to avert the course of action he seemed set on.

'You could, but you won't.' His hand moved away from her as he pressed the call button for the elevator, the firmness in his voice echoing around the large marble lobby. The elevator doors opened and he stepped inside, his handsome face set in stern lines as he looked at her. 'We do have a deal, Miss Carter-Wilson, do we not?'

Damn him, he knew she was going to say yes—had to say yes. The amusement lurking behind the darkness of his eyes showed her that. She had no other way out of the mess her father had made.

'Very well.' She joined him in the elevator, alarmed at how small it became as the doors closed and they ascended. 'But it is a deal for business, nothing else.'

'Do you think I might seduce you?' The amusement in his eyes increased and that sexy devil-may-care hint of a smile lingered at the edges of his mouth.

'Isn't that what you are renowned for, Mr Valdez?' The flirty edge to her voice was unintended and inwardly she cringed. What was it about this man that made her say and do things she never normally would? 'The waitress yesterday is testimony to that.'

He looked at her, a slight frown furrowing his brow, and she lifted her chin and glared at him. The elevator doors opened but he didn't move and she couldn't, pinned to the spot by his piercing, dark eyes.

'Is that a hint of jealousy?'

She gasped in outrage. How dared he think she was jealous, that she craved his attention? 'Absolutely not.'

Without a backward glance she flounced out of the elevator as his deep, sexy laughter chased after her. Moments later she was in a vast apartment. His apartment. His life.

* * *

Raul watched Lydia waltz into his apartment, enjoying the sway of her hips, outlined perfectly in a black skirt that hugged her body more than he suspected she'd want it to. The long black boots only emphasised her sexiness and the openness of his apartment seemed suddenly to close in on him. He'd watched many women wander around his apartment but never had he experienced the pull at emotions he kept locked away. He never let a woman close, never let her see just who he really was.

Yet somehow, Lydia had unlocked that door. He'd already told her far more about himself than he had anyone else. Was it because she was the first woman to be here for a reason other than merely sleeping in his bed? The idea of her in his bed sparked a shot of lust through him, making him want to forget the real reason she was here.

'I trust it meets with your approval,' he teased her and was rewarded with that glare of fiery passion as she turned to look at him. Would she be as inviting if his lips claimed hers in a kiss? Would she respond and match the fire of desire beginning to burn within him? He was being drawn to her by an attraction so strong even he doubted he had the power to resist its allure. But he had to—for now at least.

'Tell me, Mr Valdez, why exactly do you require my father's debt settled in such an extraordinary way when it is obvious that you have more wealth here alone than in a couple of holiday villas my father used as security?'

Was she trying to annoy him?

He moved quickly across the marble floor, his shoes tapping out an insistent rhythm as the implications of her words hit home, turning the unwanted desire into much-needed anger. 'A couple of holiday villas? Is that what you think this is about? Do you really think I am mercenary enough to call in a debt for that?'

Raul began to seriously doubt she had really grasped just how much debt her father had got himself into. It might have been to purchase holiday villas, but it was far more than a couple. He would take her straight to his office to see for herself just what her father had done and sign the contract agreed between them. The sooner he'd tied her into a contract, the better.

'That is exactly what I think. You've turned everything around and now are practically blackmailing me. I either find your brother or marry you.'

'And which would you prefer to do, *querida*?'

'Don't call me that.' The spark of fury was palpable as she stood her ground and he recalled her atrocious attempt at Spanish the night they'd first met. Then, just as now, her green eyes blazed like priceless emeralds, calling to the lustful desire within him, and he was just as adamant as ever that he would ignore it.

'We will go to my office right now and you can see for yourself exactly what your father owes, Miss Carter-Wilson.' Irritation surged through him. How dared she accuse him of underhanded dealings? He would hang on to that irritation. Use it to wipe out the idea of things he really didn't need to feel right now. Hell, why did he have to find *this* woman so sexy?

'That sounds the most sensible option,' she tossed haughtily at him, her eyes sparking defiance and her lips pressed together in a firm angry line, just begging to be kissed into submission. 'And on the way back I will check into a hotel.'

He narrowed his eyes as he looked at her. 'You don't give up, do you?'

'No, so I suggest you show me exactly what my father owes your company and I'm sure it will prove that a few days of tracing your brother will more than cover it—and release us both from the bizarre marriage deal your father must have tricked mine into agreeing to.'

'In that case, *querida*...' he took pleasure in using the endearment again, relishing the fury that shone in her eyes as much as the opportunity to remain in control of this ridiculous situation '...we shall leave immediately and sort this out.'

Her boot heels tapped on the marble floor as she walked towards him, that superior *you don't worry me* look on her face again. 'That is the most sensible thing you have said since we met in London.'

'It is a short walk to my office.' He glanced down at the sexy high-heeled boots, trying to ignore the idea of her shapely ankles encased in them and keep his thoughts firmly on the task at hand.

'A short walk will be perfect,' she said as a hint of challenge rose in those expressive green eyes.

Determined not to be affected by her, he led the way back to the elevator and out onto the busy street. Despite her heels she kept pace with him and he slowed his slightly as he entered one of the city's plazas, lined with cafés where couples enjoyed the cool winter sun of the afternoon. What would it be like to sit and relax with her, to forget the stress of their situation and get to know one another properly?

It shocked him to realise that was exactly what he wanted to do, not in the way he'd always done with other women, but in a deep and meaningful way. That would never be an option, not now. It was better if she continued to think of him as a womaniser, especially when he sensed she was not the kind of woman to indulge in one-night stands, making her exactly the kind of woman he always avoided. Was that the reason for this inconvenient attraction? Forbidden fruit? He was stronger than that, wasn't he?

He paused outside the doors of the old town building that was home to the head office of Banco de Torrez. She looked at him and the uncertainty he saw briefly in her eyes pulled at his conscience. He silenced that conscience. There was no other way of dealing with the mess created by both their fathers.

Without a word, he pushed open the large and heavy door and entered the calm interior, which, like his apartment, was modern and spacious, belying the exterior that belonged in the city's past. As he looked down at her, he saw her delicate brows rise in question and recalled her earlier remarks, suggesting that he could just write off the debt she had to pay. He could, if he was prepared to risk a company he'd built being sold off to the highest bidder. He couldn't allow that to happen to all the people who depended on Banco de Torrez for employment. The only other option was for Lydia to find Maximiliano without luring the press closer. It was time to put her *hobby* of family history to the test.

'I will show you to the office you can work from whilst here,' he said as he stepped into the elevator, trying to ignore the close proximity they were forced into once again.

Lydia followed Raul past offices where staff members worked, some greeting him and others regarding her with mild curiosity. Did they think she was his latest mistress? That thought almost made her feet stop moving, but she forced herself to continue, trying not to care what others thought.

Finally, the glass-partitioned offices finished and they reached a more private area. Raul walked in and the luxury of what was obviously his space forced her to stifle a small gasp.

'This is where you will work.' He gestured to an office area off his. She walked in, trying to ignore the way he made her feel as he stood so close, looking out of the window, which took up almost all of one wall. Rooftops of grand old buildings nestled beneath the winter sun and she wished briefly she could explore the city, get to know it better. But she was here to work, to pay off her father's debts and finally free herself of, not only Raul Valdez, but her ill-fated honour to her father. She was here ultimately for her grandmother. There wasn't time for such frivolities and most definitely not for exploring the simmering passion between them.

'Nice, but I only intend to be here for a matter of days.' She had no idea how much her father owed, but even to her ears the fact that it would only take a few days sounded extortionate. He must be desperate to trace his brother, not for any emotional reasons, she was sure, but for the money his inclusion in the business would unlock. Raul had been brutally honest about that. It must be far greater than her father owed. Much more of a lure for a cold businessman like Raul Valdez.

He shrugged casually, a move so unexpected it aroused her suspicions. What hadn't he told her?

'I think we should discuss the extent of your father's debt before you make plans to leave Madrid, because make no mistake, *querida*, you will *not* be leaving until I consider the debt repaid, either with the information I require or your signature on a marriage document.'

Inwardly, Lydia's anger surfaced. She was not his *querida*, but outwardly she remained calm and poised and she resisted the urge to reply in Spanish. She would save that pleasure for another time. 'In that case, I need to know the exact sum my father owes.'

She followed him back into his office and stood calmly waiting as he got a file out, opened it slowly and with purpose, then he looked at her as he slid it across the expanse of polished wood. The warning on his handsome face was clear and she braced herself for what was to come.

'The figure exceeds five hundred million euros.' He spoke without any emotion, any sense of surprise at the figure he mentioned. Her eyes widened in shock. How could he say that so calmly?

'And the properties used as security?' Her voice wavered and she dreaded the answer.

'Far in excess of that amount.'

How many properties had her father hidden in her name? This was much bigger than she'd imagined and with each passing hour she was getting in deeper. Too deep. It would finish her grandmother, who was recovering from a bout of ill health, if she knew how much.

'So if we married you would gain substantially

more?' He nodded and she carried on whilst she still had the strength to stand. 'Why then are you prepared to accept the deal I offered? Before I knew the extent of the sums involved, I might add.'

'I want my brother found. I'd prefer the money to come from the accounts my father set up for the purpose of his devious acts than from you and our marriage. I trust you agree.'

'I agree only on that I have no wish to get married—to you or anyone.' She injected as much confidence into her voice as she could even though inside she was still reeling from shock at the amount her father owed.

'If you agree, then you must sign this confidentiality contract.'

Suspicion nudged into her mind. What was he keeping from her? 'There must be more to it than that. What are you keeping from me, Mr Valdez?'

She stood in the middle of his office and used the long-ago-perfected art of indifference as she lifted her chin and challenged him. There was a hint of anger, a hint of bristling annoyance as his gaze met hers. Then it was gone. Replaced by icy disdain.

'You are very astute, Lydia. You should be a businesswoman.' His cutting tone bounced off her toughened barrier, but inside something changed. He'd seen her as something more than an empty-headed heiress. Briefly maybe, but he'd seen the real Lydia.

'Maybe I am,' she taunted him as she walked towards him, watching as his eyes narrowed in suspicion, noticing how his dark lashes made his eyes look so very sinfully sexy. 'Which means, before I sign any contract with you, I want to know the finer details. All of them.'

'Very well.' He moved towards her and she suddenly wished she hadn't been so bold, provoking him as she'd done moments ago, because now he was far too close. She could smell the unadulterated scent of a powerful male. It scared and excited her. 'There is one more detail which needs to be agreed upon.'

'Which is?' She looked up at him, her heart thudding at his closeness. So close that if he lowered his head he could kiss her. Where had that thought come from?

'That we become engaged—immediately.'

'No,' she snapped the word back at him, defiance echoing around the room.

'I have no wish for anyone to know that I am looking for my brother—not until I am ready. The board of directors are demanding settlement of this historic, and seriously overdue, debt, and it is imperative that they believe that we are willing to marry to clear it.'

He moved a bit closer and she bit down on her bottom lip, trying to pretend the butterflies that had begun to flutter inside her weren't because of him. She had to get a grip on herself. He couldn't know that she found him attractive. Instinctively, she knew that would be dangerous.

'Why should I care about what your board of directors think?' He'd tricked her, kept this part of the terms from her until she arrived in Madrid.

'I have until the end of December to sort this matter and in order to save thousands of jobs from being put under scrutiny or worse. There is one final clause and that is if I don't find my brother or marry you, the company will be sold. It is essential that I am seen to be dealing with the debt. It is not, after all, a small debt. I'm sure even you would agree on that.'

'And if I agree to this fake engagement?' Again she challenged him.

'You will be helping not only yourself and your father, but many hundreds of ordinary families who depend on their continued employment.'

Lydia sighed. She knew when to give in gracefully. How hard could it be to pretend to be engaged to this man? All she had to do was find his brother and then this nightmare, which was getting worse by the minute, would be over.

Raul spoke again, adding to her worries. 'And if you fail to find my brother we will have already begun the process of organising our marriage, which will have to take place on Christmas Eve.'

'You've got it all planned, haven't you?' A Christmas wedding? The thought sent panic racing through her like a torrent of flood water. She had no wish to be a married woman. She'd seen how hopeless her dreams of love and happiness were. Now Raul was reinforcing how futile those dreams were.

'I am always prepared for all eventualities.'

Why did that sound so threatening? She looked up at him, his dark eyes piercing into hers, and not a trace of anything other than seriousness was on his handsome face, nothing to soften the severity of his hard expression.

For the briefest of moments, she considered walking out. This was her father's mess and he could sort it. But she knew he never would and when it all went wrong Raul would be back, only then she would have nothing to bargain with. Not if he'd already found his brother. On top of that she could almost hear her grandmother, urging her to be strong, to get through this, as she'd always done when the fear of boarding school had been her only worry in life.

It was now or not at all and she'd do it for her grandmother's sake. Not Raul's, not hers and most definitely not her father's.

'I don't doubt that at all.' She lifted her chin defiantly, pulling herself up as a new inner strength surged through her. She'd sort this and get this man out of her life. 'But why did your father set this up?'

'To force me to accept his other son or do the one thing I have always said I wouldn't do—get married.'

'Would he really do that?'

'He would. So what is it to be, Lydia? Do we have a deal?'

She wanted to ask him how he could talk of marriage in such a detached way, but instead she took his lead and walked over to the desk, picked up the pen, and with one last angry and defiant look at him she signed the paper. 'We have a deal, Mr Valdez. I will be your fake fiancée—but only for one month.'

CHAPTER FOUR

LYDIA SAT AT her desk, her gaze fixed on the view of Madrid as the December sun set across the city, her mind wandering through the ever-increasing questions about the deal she'd struck with Raul. She twisted the large diamond engagement ring on her finger, still shocked to find it there despite having worn it for over a week.

The first ten days of the fake engagement was over and she was closer to a marriage she didn't want but would have to go through with, unless she came up with something to do with Maximiliano Valdez. She'd gone down so many dead ends this week and wasn't any closer to discovering the whereabouts of Raul's brother, or even the name he used, because she was certain it wasn't Valdez. She sighed, momentarily feeling beaten. She had to come up with something soon. It was only a matter of time before Raul demanded to know what she'd found out.

'Is your work boring you, Lydia?' Raul's deep and accented voice penetrated her thoughts and she swivelled round in her chair, turning her back on the view and her questions.

He leant casually against the door frame, his arms folded and an expression of expectancy on his face. How could he look so commanding and yet so attractive at the same time?

'I was thinking.' She tried to block that mutinous train of thought. She didn't want to think about this man like that. She mustn't.

'And are you any closer to the answer, to finding my brother?' He seemed to loom over her, his height darkening the light and airy office and, even worse than that, her heart was thudding. Was it panic that she hadn't yet got any real leads as to where his brother might be or because he was so close and she was excruciatingly aware of him?

His brows flicked up in question when she didn't respond, his eyes, so very dark, fixing her to the spot. 'Anything?'

'No.' She didn't want to elaborate on it, all too aware that now she had just over two weeks before he could demand that she became his wife and settle the debts her father had recklessly created. If she didn't find his brother, she had no other way of paying even a part of what was owed. She might have her own business, but it was still in its infancy and would never be in the league of Raul's high-earning business—or her father's debt.

He inhaled deeply, as if he was holding back on

saying something, and strode to stand at the window, his arms folded defensively across his broad chest. She watched him as the silent seconds ticked by, drawn to the width of his shoulders and the shirt that strained over his muscled arms. Strong and safe arms.

She blinked in shock. Where had that come from? She looked down at her desk, making a show of stacking papers tidily, anything other than look at this virile specimen of masculinity that threatened everything she thought she was.

'Then I am afraid we have to put in motion our alternative option.' The coolness of his voice sent a shock of fear through her as if she'd just dipped her toes into the cold seas around England.

'What alternative option?' Had she missed something?

He turned to look at her, that dark and yet strangely sexy look in his eyes, and she felt the simmer of attraction build. Damn the man. Did he know what he was doing? Was he deliberately trying to disarm her?

'To go ahead with the marriage.' His voice held a note of determination despite the calm, soft tone.

'But there are three more weeks yet.' She knew she sounded panicked, but she couldn't help it. Quickly she tried to regain her inner strength, her ability to come somewhere close to matching this man's power.

'*Sí*, that is true, but, as far as your father's debt is

concerned, we have to be seen to be preparing for marriage in order to make the repayment of that debt.'

'By who?' she fired back at him angrily.

He moved to her desk, placed his palms on it and leant towards her. 'By the board of directors, the people who have the power to insist that the contract your father signed is adhered to, that his debt is repaid by our marriage and subsequent transfer to me of those properties around the globe you claim to know nothing of.'

He was angry; she could feel it reverberating from him and bouncing off the clean white walls of the office. She'd spoken to her solicitor, knew that her father had been advised against signing such a contract, which made it all the worse. Her father had engineered the terms just to keep himself out of trouble, placing her in the firing line. Still she couldn't help but goad this proud and powerful man.

'And you always do as you are told?' Mischief entered her voice and, briefly, she had the upper hand.

He leant lower to her, his face so close to hers that if anyone was looking in through the large window such a move could be mistaken for a lover's kiss. She held her breath, refusing to back down, refusing to lose the upper hand she had inadvertently gained.

'Do you really think I would marry you—or anyone—simply because I have been told to do so?' The words were deep and accented, his breath warm on her face, his dark eyes granite hard and fixed on hers.

No, she didn't think that at all. In fact, it had crossed her mind more than once why such a commanding and in-control man would follow the wishes of his father's will so succinctly.

She leant daringly forward, closer to him and looked into the fierceness in his eyes. 'No, I don't, so maybe now would be a good time to tell me exactly what this is all about instead of waiting three more weeks and forcing us into a marriage neither of us want. I have no wish to spend the next two years with you.'

He didn't answer. His eyes searched hers, what for she didn't know, but she couldn't help the tingle that covered her lips as if his had touched hers, brushed over them and teased them—teased her—into passionate life.

She jolted back on her chair. 'What is it all about, Raul?'

A smug smile of satisfaction teased at the lips she'd just imagined kissing hers and heat spread over her cheeks. She stood up from the desk, as calmly as she could even though her insides were somersaulting wildly as she fought, once again, the pull of attraction for this proud Spaniard.

'You know it all, Lydia.'

'I'm going home,' she announced sternly, but the questioning rise of his brows left her in no doubt of her mistake.

'By home, you mean, my home?' The deep sensuous accent did untold things to her already disturbed equilibrium.

'I have never had the luxury of calling any one place home for long. Any place I stay becomes my home—temporarily at least.' Why had she said that? Why had she given away a part of her like that? Angrily, she turned and picked up her jacket and purse.

'Join me for a drink—on the way home.' His accent had deepened, become more noticeable and far too sexy.

She turned and looked at him, the challenge in his eyes unmistakable. He expected her to refuse, to run from whatever it was that had just zinged subtly between them, changing everything. Well, she'd show him he didn't scare her, that she had the power to resist the attraction—resist him.

She smiled at him brightly. 'That would be the perfect end to the day.'

The fire in Lydia's eyes did something to him as he looked at her and Raul suddenly had the urge to spend an evening with her. A long evening. Whatever it was that had reared up like a stallion between them as he'd looked into her eyes now called to him, daring him to accept the challenge this woman presented, daring him to take what he wanted. She was a challenge he shouldn't accept.

He sat opposite Lydia at a café in one of the city's most vibrant plazas, content that here they would be noticed, their status as an engaged couple brought to the attention of Madrid's society—and subsequently Carlos, who would inform the board, who were pushing more strongly for settlement of her father's debt. This would buy them both time.

He ordered wine and tapas and sat back, enjoying the buzz of early evening in Madrid, but knowing he would have to bring the conversation round to the finer details for their marriage. He'd been forced to put the marriage plan into motion because after one week it was becoming clear that maybe she wasn't able to trace his brother. Her *hobby* obviously wasn't as developed as she'd led him to believe.

'I have made the official notifications for our marriage. On Christmas Eve, you and I will marry in a civil ceremony.' She paled but before she could offer up one of her little interruptions he continued, 'Your father's debts will be cleared as soon as we are married, but we must remain living as a married couple for two years.'

'I thought we didn't have to go to the extreme of marriage.' Her eyes flashed with a spark of anger as she looked at him, calmly taking a sip of her cool white wine. Her long elegant fingers and vibrant red-painted nails drew his attention. She hadn't changed since they'd first met, just evolved into the socialite, a spoiled little heiress who had nothing better to do than pamper and indulge herself. Not at all the kind of woman he usually noticed. He liked more independent women, those who didn't read too much into a smile. So why was she getting under his skin so easily?

'Only you can decide what happens, Lydia. You need to find my brother soon. Only then can your father's debts be cleared and the marriage cancelled. Fail or take too long and the marriage will have to go ahead.'

'If I decide to do something I never fail so you shouldn't trouble yourself with all those official and legal documents just to arrange a marriage that won't be necessary.'

The defiant and determined look in her eyes stirred something deep within him, something he'd kept concealed even from himself. Annoyed at the direction of his thoughts, he pushed it aside. Far better to dislike her than desire her.

'The official arrangement to marry you on Christmas Eve is my insurance policy to ensure that you don't fail.'

'You are nothing but a blackmailer,' she threw at him and looked out of the window across the plaza. Around them an increasing amount of people were filling up the tables, their laughter and talking infusing the evening with fun and vibrancy.

'I think that particular title goes to your father.' There were moments when he believed her innocence in this, believed that she knew nothing of the properties her father had bartered with. Then, when she looked at him so defiantly, so very proudly, like an heiress who had it all and knew it, he believed nothing of the sort. She certainly gave out mixed messages.

Right now she looked vulnerable and that struck a chord within him, sent questions racing through his mind. She was gambling with far more than a few properties. Like him, she was prepared to risk her freedom, risk ending up in a marriage she didn't want. But why? She didn't appear to have a conscience for the father, a man who had used her in his scheming ways. What was keeping her here, keeping her from walking away?

'And yours,' she flung at him, the spark of fire obliterating that vulnerability. 'And I don't intend to become their victim. I will do everything I can to find your brother, Raul, everything.'

'That is very honourable of you.'

'Honour doesn't come into it. Self-preservation maybe, dislike for a man such as you, very definitely.'

'Ouch.' He laughed at her, admiring the hissing wildcat barely concealed beneath those words, thinking it would be exciting to tame her. 'Where has the little kitten gone?'

'Kitten?' She looked at him, a frown on her beautiful face.

'The one who wanted nothing more than me to kiss her as we talked at your desk.'

'I did not.' The indignation was clear in her voice as she jumped to her feet; so too was the hint of colour on her cheeks. He'd known as he'd looked at her across the desk that if he'd kissed her, if he'd followed the silent requests of her lovely full lips, he would have wanted more. He'd resisted the temptation. If he'd given in so easily he would have been living up to the reputation he'd created as part of his armour, but he'd wanted to—badly.

'Sit down, Lydia. It will look as if we are as far from lovers as can be if you stand there glaring at me so intently.'

'Which is exactly what we are.' The words hissed at him, but she did at least sit down again.

'I intend for us to be seen as, if not lovers, at least friends. We are about to enter into the happy state of marriage.'

'Hah.' The false laugh that slipped so easily from her lips left him in no doubt that she too had little sentiment for marriage. 'Is there such a thing?'

'From that I deduce your parents' marriage was as unhappy as that of my parents.' Why was he talking of such things with her? He never discussed his childhood, never talked to anyone about the cold and heartless home he'd grown up in, or the constant warring of his parents as his father's indiscretions became ever more frequent and ever more public. His mother had never forgiven the double life her husband had led for over eight years of their marriage and he intended to keep his search for the child of that double life from her for as long as possible.

'It is not me who has a half-sibling to trace.'

So the kitten's claws were still unsheathed. Maybe he should have kissed her when he'd had the chance.

'True. But would you really know? Can you really say that your father has not sired another child when you spent most of your childhood with your grandparents until you went to boarding school?'

'How do you know so much about me?' Now he had her full attention.

'Did you really expect me to even consider marrying you without some background, something more than our dinner-party talk ten years ago? Your father has told me much.'

She looked at him shrewdly, her green eyes almost dark with suspicion. 'And what did you discover?'

'That maybe you are not the spoilt little rich girl you want people to believe you are.' Now he had her attention. Her eyes blazed a furious challenge at him and who was he to refuse?

'Which means?'

'Which means, Lydia, I know you have no other choice. That at least was very clear from what he told my legal representative. Even so, we have a deal, one you will honour with either marriage or success in finding my half-brother.' He paused, letting the information sink in whilst he pushed his suspicion that there was something else, some other reason for her compliance, to the back of his mind.

'For now, that means acting as if we are preparing to unite in marriage, that we at least like each other. I have no wish for the board to pick up on any reluctance from either of us. They must not question that the debt will be settled in full, however that might be.'

'All this to save your business.' She shook her head in disbelief and it grated on him that she thought his motives for demanding the marriage appear to take place were purely selfish.

'And to save your father from ruin as well as safeguard our much-wanted state of being single.'

'Do you really expect me to believe that?'

'Sí, querida, I do.' The words he'd just spoken weren't lost on him. They were words he'd no intention of saying to any woman.

Lydia looked at Raul as he sat quietly, their little spat over. Around them the noise of the evening increased and a party atmosphere prevailed. The night was still young but she didn't have time to think of parties and fun. She had to find his brother and the turn of conversation, however fiery, had showed just how she could do that.

'I need to talk to your mother. She must know something.' That got his attention.

His dark eyes held hers and he looked up at her,

then back out to the now busy plaza, ablaze with Christmas lights. Around them the place was full of laughter and voices, the sounds echoing up around them, making everything seem surreal. She looked at the firm set of his jaw, the fierce profile, and knew she'd touched a nerve. A very raw nerve.

'I have no wish to involve my mother in this.' Finally, he turned back to face her and she could see the coldness in his eyes. 'She knows nothing of the terms of the will and that is exactly how it will stay.'

'It may be that she has the initial lead which will help with this. After all, she was married to your father. She must know something of what happened.'

'Why do you say that?' His icy voice was full of disdain but she pushed on regardless. She had no intention of ending up married to this man in three weeks' time. By Christmas she'd be back in London and if it meant upsetting him and his mother was the only way out of it then that was exactly what she would do.

'Women usually know. I have also worked out, from the small amount of information you have given me, that you and your brother must have been born within months of each other.' She ploughed on, regardless of the deepening anger on his face. This wasn't a time for sentimental feelings of guilt. This was a time to save herself from a marriage she had no wish to make.

'Which is exactly why I have no wish to drag her into it. Imagine how it must have felt to be a new mother and know your husband was sleeping with another woman, that you'd provided the much-needed heir and were now surplus to requirements.'

Her temper boiled at the thought of the man who'd done that to his wife, Raul's mother, and then a flash of sympathy for Raul himself. Had he too grown up knowing he was merely the heir required and not the son much wanted? Was that why he was so hard, so cold and unreachable?

She pushed it aside. 'We have no other option, Raul, so when you have decided which way to proceed, perhaps you will be good enough to let me know.' She stood up and began to walk away, aware of him behind her, tossing notes onto their table and following her.

She didn't wait. She walked into the plaza, wanting only to get away from him.

'I am not accustomed to women walking away from me,' he stated harshly as he caught up with her. Did he expect her to bend to his wishes, do his bidding exactly as he wanted? No, she would never do that. She'd seen her own mother do it and then seen her leave, unable to tolerate the bullying regime any longer; she hadn't even cared that she was leaving behind her daughter. It had been her grandmother who'd looked after her from then on.

She stopped to look up at Raul, an uncomfortable thought settling over her. For the first time in her life she wondered if she too should have been the required heir or even the much-sought-after son. Had she been a disappointment and let-down to both her parents when she'd arrived? A daughter neither of them had wanted?

Suddenly her childhood made so much more sense. Bitterness swept over her and she responded, lashing out at the man who'd brought such a realisation about.

'Well you are about to find out what it's like. I'm not staying here whilst you dither about just who you want to help with finding your brother. It seems to me you would rather marry than find him. What are you afraid of, Raul? Sharing your inheritance?'

He grabbed her wrist and pulled her close against him, looking directly into her eyes. For a brief moment she thought she saw desire combined with the anger her words had induced. Her heart thumped wildly in her chest, his closeness invading every sense in her body as drops of rain began to unceremoniously fall.

He didn't care about the rain, or that they were quickly getting wet, instead he looked into her eyes, his breath as hard and fast as hers. Did he feel that powerful attraction too? The same attraction she was fighting? She couldn't allow him to know what he did to her.

'Let me go,' she demanded fiercely, wanting only

to hide the spark of something very close to desire that had leapt to life inside her, despite the dousing by the rain.

She couldn't break eye contact as the rain began to fall harder; locals and tourists alike sought refuge inside the buildings of the plaza, but she couldn't move. It was as if he'd cast a spell, fixed her to the spot. She couldn't walk away, didn't want to move.

He let her hand go, but remained so very close, looming over her like a matador, and to her horror she still couldn't move, couldn't back away from him. Around them the plaza had emptied, the noise of the pre-Christmas parties replaced by the constant thud of rain onto the now soaked bricks and cobbles of the plaza. She could feel him so very close, feel the heat of his body, smell his masculine scent. For good- ness' sake, she could even taste his kiss, taste what it would be like to have his lips pressed against hers.

Her hair was beginning to stick to her head, her jacket to her skin. She began to shiver, but she wasn't cold. Far more powerful sensations were rac- ing round her body. Raul pulled off his jacket, his eyes locked on hers all the time as he placed it round her shoulders. It made it worse. She could smell him around her, feel his heat caressing her, and as the rain quickly soaked him his shirt became tantalisingly transparent, serving only to heighten his strength and masculinity—not to mention her barely veiled desire to be kissed by him.

Before she knew what she was doing or had time to think of the implications of such actions, she'd moved closer still. It was all the invitation he'd needed and within seconds she was in his arms, her own wrapped around his neck as his lips, hard and demanding, claimed hers. Her wet body clung to his, the sensation of being against him so wildly sensual as the rain continued to fall on them that she couldn't help the sigh of pleasure escaping.

His husky whisper in Spanish only added to the electrifying moment and she couldn't stop herself pressing closer still, feeling every hard contour of his body against hers.

Then sense prevailed. What was she doing? Kissing the one man she shouldn't kiss. Her enemy. What was the matter with her?

'That,' she breathed heavily as she pulled back from him and out of his arms, the rain still pounding down around them. 'That was not part of our deal.'

'Yet you can't maintain you didn't want me to kiss you, can you, *querida*?'

She shook her head as he continued. 'In fact, it was you who started it, you who moved towards me. What is a man meant to do when a woman like you kisses him? Stand there and not move?'

'I am not your *querida*.' She hurled the words at him, glaring accusingly as her heart thumped and her body pulsed with need.

'So you have said.'

'I don't want anything from you, Raul, and especially not a kiss. All you need to do is find out if your mother has any idea who it was your father had an affair with.' Desperate to rid her body of the heat that surged powerfully through it after that explosive kiss, she pulled off his jacket, allowing the rain to cool her, to dampen the desire she hadn't been able to fight.

'That may not be easy.' He glared at her, obviously fighting the same desire as she was. A man like Raul Valdez, who had a reputation for being as ruthless a lover as a businessman, surely wouldn't have to fight the attraction.

'Marrying you won't be easy either.' She spoke the truth, but now those words came from a different place than they had done when she'd first met him. She hadn't known then just how lethal a kiss from him could be.

'Very well,' he said as he looked down at her, raindrops falling from his hair, making her want to reach up and push it back from his forehead. 'I will arrange for you to meet my mother. And now I suggest we go and get dry—separately.'

'Absolutely separately. There won't be a repeat of this. Of that much I can assure you.'

CHAPTER FIVE

THE LAST THING Lydia had expected was Raul to announce they were going away for the weekend and to be driven out of Madrid, into the countryside. Even more of a shock was the fact that he had relented and agreed to take her to see his mother. In the short time she'd spent with Raul, Lydia knew he didn't do anything on a whim. Everything had a purpose. So what was this visit all about?

The question lingered in her mind until finally, after what had felt like hours of driving, due to the tension filling the car, he turned off the road. The car tyres scrunched over the gravel drive of a country villa, typically Spanish in every way. Not at all like the grandeur of his Madrid penthouse apartment.

'This is nice,' she said lightly as he turned off the engine, silence filling the car, blending with that ever-present tension as he looked at her. She'd been acutely aware of his presence next to her, of every move he'd made as he'd driven first on the busy roads away from the city and then to the quieter and smaller roads through farmland, interspersed with villages.

'My weekend retreat,' he offered as he got out of the car. She watched him walk around the front of it and towards her door, rebelliously enjoying the view of his long legs and lean body encased, as always, in a suit, which did little to hide his strength. Memories of how it had felt to be pressed against his body as rain had soaked them rushed back at her, adding to the air of expectancy zinging between them.

Aware he would think she was waiting for him to open her door, she quickly did so herself and slipped out of the low sports car. Standing outside in the fresh air of winter, she expected to feel less intimidated by him, but after the previous night and the kiss that had set fire to her whole body she was anything but. There wasn't any escape from the attraction, no relief from the sizzle of tension now.

She couldn't allow herself to be drawn in by it— by him. She had to keep in mind his motives for bringing her to Spain, to this romantic villa. It was purely money and wealth that drove him; not the need to find a brother he'd never known of, purely money. He might have all the trappings of wealth, but other than that he was no different from Daniel, wanting her for what she had, not who she really was.

'And your mother lives here?' She hoped the question was light and casual, belying the turmoil in her mind, but the look he fired her way was far from that. It was cold and calculating. Distanced yet intense.

'No, she lives about half an hour's drive into the hills.'

So she was alone with him again and this time there wouldn't be an office to escape to. 'I see.'

'You made yourself perfectly clear last night, Lydia. You have nothing to fear from being here with me.' The brusqueness of his voice backed up his words and she tried not to be disappointed as a small reckless part of her wanted him to kiss her again— and much more. She pushed that woman aside. She had to remain strong and as detached as he evidently was. It was the only way.

'So we are here purely to see your mother?'

'*Sí.* Did you think I had ulterior motives for bringing you here?' Raul's dark eyes fixed her to the spot, but the haughty façade she lived behind served her well.

'Only to increase your wealth.'

He stepped towards her, but she stood firm, retained her cool composure. 'All I want, Lydia, is for you to find my brother. Then I can secure the future of the company by settling the extortionate debts *your* father has run up and move forward in my life.'

Before she could register his words, he turned and walked towards the door of the villa. Deep within her, hidden expertly away, she trembled with shock. It might be her father's debts he wanted repaid, but he'd just confirmed he was no better than either his father or hers. This was all about greed.

He opened the door and stepped back for her to enter the villa, which was not at all what she'd expected of this hard and dominating businessman. This was more like a home. It was comfortable and welcoming, not a sleek modern angle in sight. It was the kind of place she would choose, the kind of place to finally put down roots.

Her early years had been spent moving from one house to the next. She'd never had time to settle, time to make friends before the family was on the move again. Then, if that wasn't unsettling enough, her mother had left her with her father. Luckily her grandmother had stepped in and her father had been all too ready to allow her to live with her grandmother, the only time she'd felt she belonged.

She pushed away that yearning need to make a place a home, to actually belong somewhere, and focused her attention on the reason for being here in the first place. To ensure her grandmother didn't find out just how low her own son had sunk.

'Then I suggest the sooner I can speak with your mother, the better. Time is ticking away and as I have no intention at all of marrying you in three weeks' time I want my father's debt settled.' She tried to hide her see-sawing emotions and appear as calm as he was, watching as he moved around the villa, looking out of place in his smart suit. The ruthless businessman she'd come to know didn't fit here at all.

'You will not ask her anything directly.' Raul's firm voice snapped in the air around them like the first clap of thunder as a storm broke.

'Then how am I supposed to fulfil my part of the deal?' What was he trying to hide or, more to the point, what didn't he want her to know?

'My parents' marriage was an arranged one and even as a young child I sensed the undercurrent of dislike between her and my father. They barely tolerated one another.' Each word was emotionless and matter-of-fact. Exactly how she would describe her childhood and attempt to hide the hurt emotions of the child that still remained. Was Raul hurting too? Could it be that he was more capable of emotions than he wanted her to believe?

'That is a scenario I am familiar with.' She dropped the words in casually as she looked around the villa, liking it more with each passing second.

He looked at her as he walked across the room and opened doors to the terrace, the cool air of winter rushing in, fresh and stimulating. When his eyes met hers seconds later, that mask of indifference was well and truly in place. 'My father led a double life, Lydia. For eight years he had two families.'

When she didn't speak he continued, 'I was sent to boarding school from a very young age and never knew family life. When I came home it was to hostilities and stand-offs. Then one day he was gone. So although I assume my mother knows all about the affairs my father had after that, as well as the mistress he'd lived with and had a family with alongside ours, I would rather she didn't have to face it head-on.'

'Fine,' she said as she watched him, tall and powerful against the backdrop of the rural room of the villa. 'I will find a way to enquire about Max without being too obvious.'

'You will also leave her in no doubt that we are lovers. I don't want her to find out what my father has done—ever.'

'Why did he do it? Set the terms of his will like that?'

'He obviously thought I was like him and that I would not tolerate sharing the success of the business with anyone. I suspect he thought I would find an enforced marriage more preferable.' The bitterness in his voice was clear, but deep down she didn't believe he was like that.

He looked at her, his eyes locking with hers for a moment, then walked out through the open doors onto a terrace that boasted a pool, covered now for the colder winter months, and, beyond that, stunning views of the countryside.

She watched as he walked across the terrace, saw the tension in his shoulders when he stood with his back to her, rigid and upright; sympathy filled her. She knew what it was like to grow up in a home where parents didn't even know the meaning of the word marriage, let alone love. Such an upbringing had made her yearn for love and happiness, a desire that had led to one disastrous relationship and now this, a fake engagement. Would she ever find love? Did it really exist?

'Won't it hurt your mother more when she finds out our relationship is fake?' She walked out onto the terrace, the chill of the afternoon making her shiver. Or was it the coldness coming from the man who'd kissed her so passionately she'd nearly gone up in flames?

'That is a risk I am prepared to take.' He turned to face her, the set of his jaw hard and angular. 'I'd rather she thinks my engagement failed when we go back to our lives than learn the full extent of my father's deceit and treachery.'

'As you wish.'

'It goes without saying that whatever you discover must never become common knowledge, something which you agreed to adhere to in the contract.' He turned to face her, hard lines of worry on his brow. He still didn't trust her, even though she was doing this to clear her name and her father's debts.

'You don't trust me at all, do you?'

'I never trust anyone, Lydia. Trust is like love— an empty word that people pretend to believe in.'

'Do you really believe that?' She couldn't believe the venom of his words.

'I do, but I have no wish to discuss it.' He walked from the room and she knew he meant it; the discussion was over. She only hoped his mother was easier to talk to. The sooner she found out the name his brother might be using, the sooner she could walk away from Raul and his unyielding presence.

By the time they had finished the meal with his mother later that evening, Raul was beginning to think that maybe he could trust Lydia. For the entire evening she'd put on a brilliant show of being his fiancée. She'd acted to perfection the part of a woman who loved him and wanted to be with him for the rest of her life. She'd even convinced his mother that their chance meeting just a short while ago was lovers' fate as she'd excitedly shown her the engagement ring.

'I never thought I would see the day my son fell in love.' His mother's words, said in heavily accented English. Her enthusiasm for their happiness grated on his conscience and guilt nudged at him for the lies he had told her and the lies still yet to come. He'd told Lydia he'd rather his mother think their romance had ended than know the truth, but now, seeing the happiness on her face, he wasn't so sure.

'When is the wedding?' his mother asked as she sipped at her wine.

'Christmas Eve.' Despite Lydia's subtle scrutiny, he managed to say it calmly, but didn't miss the question on his mother's face.

'Why the rush?' For a moment she grappled with her limited English.

He took Lydia's hand and looked into her eyes. 'I met the woman I love. Why wait?'

Lydia held his gaze, blushing prettily and very convincingly, then smiled up at him. A warm smile that lit up her eyes, sending those sparks of lust hurtling through him once more as memories of their kiss in the rain surfaced.

'We want to be married and, as neither of us wants a big fancy affair with lots of guests, Christmas Eve seemed perfect.'

'Then you are not…?' His mother's question died away as he turned his attention to her, pulling Lydia close against him.

'No. Goodness.' Lydia laughed and the relief on his mother's face shocked him. Did she suspect there was more to this engagement than love? Worse still, did she somehow know what his father had done with his will? She might have been a distant figure in his childhood, thanks to his father's influence, but she was still his mother and that counted for something at least. He had no wish to hurt her.

'We want to marry, as soon as possible and with the minimum of fuss.' He spoke first in fast Spanish, to ensure his mother understood, then repeated it in English as he looked at Lydia.

'And we'd like you to be there,' Lydia enthused and Raul inwardly groaned as she got carried away with the role she was acting out. One more bit of deceit to extricate himself from.

'I will be.' His mother smiled then hugged them both in turn. He watched as Lydia hugged her back, recalling the little she'd told him of her childhood. She had painted a very cold picture. Had she missed out on a mother's love?

'There is one other person we'd like at the wedding,' Lydia said softly, almost absently. Her skills for acting were very convincing. He'd have to be wary of that.

'I think I know who that might be.' His mother responded to Lydia but looked at him and he had the strange sensation of being out of control, completely at another person's mercy, something he'd long ago decided never to be again. 'His name is Maximiliano, after his father.'

To hear it confirmed—from his mother—hurt like hell. He had never been the son his father had wanted, even from the moment he'd been born. The honour of being given his father's name had been bestowed on the son he'd truly wanted.

'Do you know where we can find him?' Lydia asked, not taking her attention from his mother once. Could she sense his anger, his growing dislike for a brother he'd never known, the only son his father had wanted?

She shook her head and changed the conversation immediately to something completely different, preferring to indulge in a conversation about village life, and Raul knew the opportunity had passed. He shook his head at Lydia as she looked up at him. He didn't want his mother hounded about this. It obviously made her as angry as it made him.

He'd lost his father and she'd lost her husband. Of course she didn't want to bring her husband's love child into their lives now and she most certainly wouldn't want him at her son's wedding. No, this wasn't the way to find out about his brother.

'We need to go back to the villa,' he said, smiling at his mother, trying to ignore the shocked look on Lydia's face. He would have to find another way of tracing his brother. He was not going to have his mother's life turned upside down just because his father had made one last dig at both of his sons, pitching them against each other.

He guided Lydia towards the door, wanting to leave before something more was said to upset his mother, and was standing beneath the archway, which in summer became covered in bougainvillea, when his mother called to Lydia, who exchanged a glance with him then went back to see her. He waited, not wanting to see the moment when his mother would be duped once more into thinking he and Lydia were in love. A few minutes later, Lydia reappeared, looking as uncomfortable as he felt. At least she had a conscience.

He wanted to ask her what had been said, but

decided against it. In a few weeks the fake engagement would be over and whatever it was wouldn't matter any more.

Lydia had clutched her small bag in her lap as Raul had navigated the twisty turns of the road back to his villa, aware that she was now holding the key to her freedom. His mother had pushed an old envelope into her hands and the words she'd spoken in heavily accented English still collided with Lydia's conscience. She should have put the woman at ease and spoken Spanish, but she was still uneasy about doing so after Raul's put-down and she wasn't yet ready to prove to him she was anything other than an empty-headed party girl.

She stood now, looking out over the dark countryside, wondering what exactly was in the envelope and why his mother had kept it from him all along. She'd have to wait until she was alone. The last thing she wanted to do was unleash the secret until she knew what it was and if it would help her find Raul's brother. She had to know if it really did reveal enough to enable her to walk away from Raul, her father's debts cleared. She could still hear his mother's words as she'd thrust the envelope into her hands, struggling to put what she wanted to say into English. Her eyes, as dark as her son's but much softer, had implored Lydia to listen, to hear what she had to say. It was the kind of look that crossed any language barrier.

'I have guarded this secret from my son since the day he was born and now, as the woman he loves, it is your secret to guard—or share.'

'What wise words did my mother give you?' Raul's voice made her jump as he came up behind her. His nearness set off the thudding in her heart and she tried to tell herself it was because of the secret she now held and definitely not because of the man.

'You startled me,' she said as she whirled round to face him, finding herself just that little bit too close. He looked down at her, questions and suspicion brimming in his eyes.

Today she'd seen a very different man from the hard businessman she'd first met in London and her thoughts towards him were changing. Just like her, he had every reason to portray a tough exterior to the world. But knowing this made her vulnerable to him and, worse, made it dangerous being close to a man she was undeniably attracted to. Apart from that kiss last night, she'd kept her distance and her sanity, but now, holding the key to his past and to her freedom, her resistance had slipped a little lower.

'Did she tell you anything more about my brother?' His words were soft and coaxing but fierceness in his eyes betrayed his emotions more clearly than she was certain he would have wanted.

'No, she didn't tell me anything about your brother.' Lydia embellished the truth, not liking having to lie, but until she knew what was in that envelope she couldn't tell him. Partly to protect him but more out of respect for whatever it was that his mother had concealed. She must have had a good reason for doing it, but as soon as Lydia knew she would tell him and then hopefully free herself of this ridiculous contract.

'She must have said something.' His dark eyes narrowed in suspicion and she glanced at her bag as it lay on the table behind him, holding the information about his brother that they both needed to know. For her it was freedom and for him it was nothing but gaining yet more wealth.

'She believes we are in love, Raul,' she said and walked away from him, needing to create some space around her. She needed to think and find a way to hide the ever-increasing attraction that had far more to do with a genuine interest in him than the spark of lust-filled desire he had referred to. 'She just wanted to wish us well and make sure I knew how happy she was that you'd found someone to love.'

His eyes narrowed and he said something under his breath in Spanish. Something she understood.

She thinks I love you?

Lydia ignored the stab of hurt that rushed through her. 'Of course, I didn't enlighten her to the fact that neither of us believes in love at all.'

'This is going to hurt her, when we don't go through with the marriage.' He dragged his fingers through his hair, distracting her for a moment from her misgivings, and she tried to focus her mind as he continued in that sexy accent. 'I didn't want that.'

'Then perhaps you should tell her the truth and ask outright if she knows just who her husband was seeing, who the mother of his other son is?'

He turned to glare at her. 'My father kept another woman's presence and that of his child from my mother. I do not think she will tell us anything.'

'But she might know something.' Lydia tried to keep the desperation from her voice. She had to find his brother. The alternative was just too much to contemplate.

'No. My father deceived her in the worst possible way—and me.'

'Maybe this clause in his will is his way of making amends.' Lydia clutched at futile straws of hope, trying to smooth the roughened waters they were now on. 'Maybe he's trying to force you together, to accept one another.'

'It is a last chance of having a stab at the son he never really wanted.' Raul's voice became a growl as he tried to keep his anger in check and deep down she knew his pain. She'd been the daughter her mother and father had not wanted and the only child her mother had carried to term. She knew all about not being wanted.

Despite this she knew he was thinking out loud and for a moment she wanted to tell him about the envelope in her bag. Wouldn't he want to know its contents? She almost relented, but if she gave it to him wouldn't that give him all the power once more, when all she wanted to do was get out of the farce of an engagement and back to her life—as a single woman?

'Well, whatever it is, it's a mess I intend to get myself out of.' She spoke forcibly, trying to instil confidence into herself. She had to find a way out of this engagement. She couldn't risk ending up married to such a cold, unemotional man and, if this was it, she wasn't prepared to tell him yet.

'As do I. If you haven't come up with something within the next few days, then we will have to build on our show of an engagement. Start making more definite plans.'

'Won't that give your mother false hope? After all, neither of us plans to go through with this marriage.'

'Right now I would rather she discover that we are not in love and not getting married than discover the true extent of my father's treachery.'

'What is it you have in mind?' she asked suspiciously, not liking the calculated way his mind worked.

'We will be seen out in Madrid next week, but the best opportunity to bring a flourishing affair to the attention of the board will be at a thirtieth wedding anniversary party being given by one of them and, knowing the couple concerned, it will be a lavish affair, attended by the elite of Madrid's society.

A chance for you to indulge in your favoured pastime of shopping.'

'I see, so I am to be paraded around like one of your conquests.'

'No. You will be on my arm as my intended bride. A very different thing from a conquest.' There was smugness in his voice. Damn the man. He knew exactly how to get the upper hand.

'As you wish. I will, as always, do my job to the best of my ability.' The haughty words flew from her lips and she glared challengingly at him, daring him to disagree.

'That is all I ask for, Lydia.'

'Is it?' She looked hard at him, trying to forget that all-consuming kiss they'd shared in Madrid, the kiss that, if she hadn't put a stop to it, would have become something they both wanted but couldn't have. There was no place in their so-called engagement for desire or passion. None whatsoever.

He moved towards her, making her heart leap. '*Sí*, Lydia, it is.'

She sidestepped him. 'Then I will say goodnight.'

For a moment she thought he was going to say something else, but instead he just smiled, that soft, seductive smile he'd used in his office just hours before she'd all but begged him to kiss her. 'Goodnight, Lydia.'

Before she could change her mind, she grabbed her purse from the table and went to her room. She closed the door and sat on her bed, taking out the old, yellowed envelope and looking at it for a few moments.

Finally, she opened it, the paper crinkling as she did so. It was in Spanish and she was thankful of her studies. His mother had hired a private investigator and his typewritten reports of Raul's father's whereabouts contained all she needed to track Max down.

She was free. They were free. She should tell Raul.

She walked to the door and was about to open it, but paused. What would he think when she went to look for him after the underlying tension in all he'd said before she'd come to her room? Would he think that she wanted to carry on from their kiss? No, she couldn't risk that, not after the way she had all but begged him to kiss her, to hold her close. A fierce blush rushed over her cheeks as she recalled the way she'd clung to him, pressing her body against his so wantonly.

She couldn't risk a repeat of that kiss. She had to hold on to the fact that she had all she needed to free herself of Raul Valdez and, if she wanted to, blow his controlled world apart.

CHAPTER SIX

THE INFORMATION RAUL'S mother had handed to her had been a shock, but exactly what she needed. For the last five days Lydia had kept it to herself as she'd completed her search. Now she was finally ready to tell Raul, but with the anniversary party only a few hours away she didn't know if it was the right time. She should be elated, overjoyed that the fake engagement they had entered into was not going to end with an alarmingly real two-year marriage, but the thought of coldly delivering all she now knew and walking away didn't feel right.

What was the matter with her? Two weeks ago she would have willingly hurled abuse at the hard and tough exterior that was Raul Valdez. At first, her intention had been to find out where his brother was, then deliver the information coldly. She'd wanted to make him feel as insignificant as he'd made her feel all those years ago when they'd first met. That evening had haunted her ever since, making her squirm with embarrassment each time she recalled it. Despite her desire to make him feel as insignificant, it wasn't what she wanted to do now.

Something had changed. She'd glimpsed briefly beneath that hardness and seen a very different man. The kind of man who warmed her heart and made it skip a beat. The kind of man she found attractive and she was sure that this time he was not as indifferent to her as he had once been. Not if that kiss in the rain was anything to go by.

'It is time to leave.' Raul's firm tone dragged her from her thoughts, making her instantly question if she truly had seen a different man from the powerful and controlled man who stood before her, resplendent in his tuxedo.

He looked devastatingly handsome, pulling her already stretched nerves tighter as she fought to conceal the effect he had on her. The black tuxedo hugged his body, fitting him to perfection and highlighting his strength, and the white of his shirt emphasised the olive tones of his skin. But it was his face that really made her heart flutter. The sultry and very sexy expression in his eyes, the slight curve of a smile on his lips and the raised brows as he slowly took in every detail of her silver dress filled her with excitement.

'We should talk.' She tried to concentrate, to focus on the here and now, but nerves skittered round her. Why did she feel so nervous? It wasn't as if tonight were a real date. She stepped towards him, trying to still the thud of her heart and be herself, but something had changed and that something had happened as she'd kissed him in the rain. Since then everything had been different. She'd been trying to ignore it but as she looked up at him she knew she couldn't any longer—didn't want to.

'Not now.' His incredibly sexy voice filled with control and command, but she had to tell him. She didn't want any more hidden secrets.

'But there are things—'

'Later.' He cut across her appeal. The determination in that word and the hard, feral look he gave her almost silenced her, but he needed to know what she'd found out. She couldn't keep it from him. It wasn't just because it meant they no longer had to continue with the charade of their engagement. It was something else, something much deeper, something she'd never expected to find. She pushed the thought aside. She would be totally out of her depth with this man if she indulged in such notions. Whatever it was between them it was merely lust. A strong sexual attraction. Nothing more.

'No, we must talk, now, before we go to the party.' She hated that she sounded so pleading but, now that she knew for sure the truth about his brother, he had to know. Not that it changed anything for her, but it would definitely change things for Raul.

'Lydia, we are already late. We leave now. After

all, we have to convince everyone our engagement is real, do we not?'

'B-but…' she stammered over the word, unable to believe how she'd ever imagined a hidden vulnerable side to him.

'Now, Lydia. I have timed our arrival to maximum effect. Whatever you have to say can wait.'

'Very well, let's go.' She picked up her small silver clutch bag, which matched the glitz of the stunning dress she'd bought that afternoon. She should have been ecstatic to find such a dress and the contact she'd made with the designer for her own boutiques, but the contents of the envelope had been weighing heavily on her mind. They still were.

Raul's silence as they drove through the busy streets of Madrid to one of the most prestigious hotels was difficult to say the least. He'd made it clear he didn't want to talk of anything, that arriving with maximum impact and creating a couple newly engaged was all he cared about.

Now, as she entered the large room, tables adorned with silver decorations in celebration of the couple's anniversary, Raul changed. He smiled and became very attentive. He placed his hand in the small of her back, partly touching her skin due to the backless design of the dress, and she caught her breath as a frisson of awareness raced up her spine.

She turned to look up at him and the smile of satisfaction that lingered on his lips only heightened that awareness. For the briefest of moments, his dark gaze locked with hers, desire surging through the normal granite hardness.

'A very convincing act, *querida*.' His voice was deep and so very sexy that she couldn't break that eye contact even though she wanted to. 'Now it must be continued as we greet our hosts.'

Raul guided her through the glamorous guests and she was aware of the curious glances cast their way. Either Raul was such a playboy that nobody expected him to settle to marriage or she was very different from the kind of woman he usually had at his side. Whatever it was, she was far from comfortable.

She put on a smile as he introduced her in Spanish to a couple whose love for one another was more than obvious. The tall and elegant woman, named Estela, smiled at her and spoke in Spanish.

'She said you are very beautiful, an English rose.' Raul's voice broke through her thoughts, sounding so very different from the harshness he usually adopted. All part of the show, she reminded herself.

Lydia looked at the woman and replied in Spanish, 'Thank you and congratulations.'

'Your Spanish is excellent,' Estela replied with a smile and a quick glance at Raul, as if she knew what Lydia was doing.

Beside her she could feel the shockwaves coming off Raul. That dinner party, when he'd made her feel so low, so useless, was now being paid back. He said nothing and when she turned to smile at him she knew he was furious.

'You make a very handsome couple,' Estela's husband added, defusing the charged atmosphere slightly as he put his arm around his wife's shoulders and pulled her close. 'Your father knew what he was doing, Raul.'

Lydia's gaze held Raul's, but he was stoically calm, not a trace of emotion of any kind. Just how much did the board know of their arrangement? And if they knew it all, why was there any need to act the part of lovers?

As if sensing her annoyance and her questions, Raul called over a passing waiter and handed a flute of champagne to her, then his hosts and finally took one himself.

'A toast,' he said in Spanish. 'To love. Long may it last.'

Lydia raised her glass towards the couple and joined in the toast, then took a sip of the sparkling liquid, but nearly choked on the bubbles as Raul added one more toast.

'And to the English rose who will very soon be my wife.' He looked at her and the sexy rise of his brows threw a challenge at her, daring her to disagree.

Estela spoke again, her excitement clear. 'I'm looking forward to your wedding, to seeing two people so right for each other joined in marriage.'

Two people so right for each other? Was that really

how they looked? How could that be when there were so many secrets between them? So much anger?

Raul was furious. Lydia spoke Spanish—fluently? She'd been living with him for over two weeks and had not uttered a word in his language. What else was she hiding? Her ability to act a part was as good as her ability to conceal the truth.

For the last hour Raul had enjoyed having Lydia close at his side as she portrayed a woman happily engaged to him, leaving nobody in any doubt that, whilst their marriage was one that began in the boardroom of Banco de Torrez, it would definitely be continued in the bedroom.

It went against everything he believed in to admit it, but it had also stirred something within him, something deeper than merely lust or desire for a beautiful woman. It was as if they were drawn together by a connection as yet undiscovered—or was he being irrational, wanting things his childhood had shown to be impossible?

He watched her laugh with other guests, standing back to admire the sexy dress that clung like a sparkling waterfall to her body, making him want to stand beneath the cool water until he drowned. She looked amazing and there wasn't a man in the room who hadn't drunk in her beauty tonight. Her back was slightly turned to him and the daring backless dress gave him a view of soft creamy skin that he wanted to kiss and taste. Hell, he wanted a lot more than just to kiss her.

'When were you going to tell me you spoke Spanish?' he demanded as she turned to him, his annoyance at what she did to him increasing.

'You didn't ask,' she replied, reverting to English with a smile.

'Come.' The word snapped from him as he avoided being drawn in by her and dragged his thoughts back on track and away from what he would do to her if they were alone. From the way her eyes widened in surprise he had startled her with the ferocity of that one word. 'We will dance, show the cream of Madrid's society that we are uniting in marriage for more than financial gain.'

'Lie to them, you mean.' Her words were soft, her delicate accent sweet and her smile seductive, but the spark of anger in her eyes belied all she was trying to portray.

'I want to show them that we are attracted to one another. I do not think that is a lie, *querida*.' He couldn't resist taunting her with that word.

As Raul put his arms around Lydia, pulling her close against his body, a jolt of sizzling awareness sparked through him. Just what was it about this woman that made him react so acutely to her?

Her perfume invaded his senses, the sweet floral fragrance a stark contrast to the untouchable image she created in her clinging silk gown.

'What was it you wanted to tell me earlier? What other secrets have you kept from me?' He recalled her insistence at telling him something and now he was so pleased he'd waited. Whatever it was it would give him something to think of instead of focusing on the way the curves of her body moved against his as they danced. It was exquisite and torturous at the same time. Every move she made increased his awareness of her. Soon he wouldn't be able to ignore it, wouldn't be able to use conversation to hide what he truly wanted—Lydia.

'I don't think now is the time—or place.' Her eyes, so very green, met his, but he could clearly see her anxiety within them. What was she keeping from him? A trickle of icy unease slipped down his spine.

'I disagree, *querida*.'

She moved against him, chasing away that unease, and if his voice held a note of wavering control, it was much more to do with the woman in his arms than the words she spoke.

She tensed, her gaze firmly fixed on his, the spark of defiance stirring within those green depths. 'Not here, not like this.'

'Like what? Like lovers?' He knew without a doubt that she was fighting the same attraction that was hurtling through him, roughly snuffing out the unease that had dared to surface. Right at this moment, as they stood there among the party guests, the outcome of the evening was almost inevitable, but he couldn't let desire cloud his mind, distract him from what he must do.

'I need to talk to you.'

'Only talk?' he teased, enjoying the blush that swept over her face and the way she continued to dance, as if to mask the growing and very insistent attraction. 'Are you sure about that?'

She frowned, with confusion or annoyance, he wasn't sure. 'I need to talk to you about your brother.'

His brother? Now she had his attention. 'Then talk.'

'As you wish.' She'd adopted that sexy, haughty voice that seemed to beg him to take her in his arms and kiss her, but her chosen topic halted such thoughts—for now.

'Tell me.'

'When we saw your mother, she gave me an envelope as we left.'

Finally, she was going to tell him what that exchange with his mother had been all about. He'd known something had been said, known she was keeping something from him, but he'd blanked it all out, unwilling to deal with the truth, not because he wanted to go ahead with the marriage, but because he wasn't ready to look the past in the eye. Now he couldn't put it off any longer.

'And?'

'And it contained the information I needed to find your brother. Reports from a private investigator she'd hired.'

'She knew all along?' Raul couldn't hold back the shock from his voice.

'Yes, which means your worry of hurting her is unfounded. She was trying to protect you.'

'And have you found him?'

This was what he'd hoped for ever since he'd embarked on the bizarre deal with the delectable Miss Carter-Wilson. It also meant that contract would very soon be ended—as would the need to keep her close. But the past was bearing down on him.

Lydia looked at him and he sensed she was holding something back. Eventually she spoke. 'I have, yes.'

'And he is here in Madrid?'

'I believe he is living in London at the moment.'

'Then we shall go to London.'

'No. You will go to London. There is no need for me to be part of this any more.' She looked at him, her green eyes wide and round with shock.

'*Sí, querida.* Our deal will not be complete until I have met my brother.'

The spark of fury burned in her eyes and those so very kissable lips became a firm angry line.

'That's not very fair. To change the terms of our agreement like that, Raul.'

'Our agreement is to find my brother or get married. Only seeing through one of those options will unlock the funds to clear your father's debt. This is, after all, what it's all about. Your father's debt.'

'You really are quite mercenary, aren't you?'

'Are you only just realising this?' He couldn't keep the amusement from his voice. Her directness was refreshing. Nobody had ever dared to tell him that.

'Unfortunately, yes, and that's a mistake I will now pay for.'

'We will fly to London together and once I have met my brother your part of the deal will be honoured and your father's debts will be cleared.'

'And if your brother has no wish to meet you, to be part of the family business?'

Right now this all seemed too real and Raul couldn't think past the fact that Max had been found.

'Then your father's debts will be called in immediately and at the moment I only know of one other way for you to clear them.'

Lydia glared angrily at him. How could she have felt sorry for him? She'd let her guard down, allowed his charm to defuse her anger and hostility.

'Do you know anything about your brother?' She needed to gain the upper hand, to control the way this was going.

'Only that he shares my father's name.' Raul glowered at her. Had she touched a raw nerve? What would he say when she told him all she'd discovered? And more to the point, how did she tell him?

'But he had not used his surname.'

'So, he has shunned the Valdez name.' Raul's voice sounded firm and full of irritation. 'When exactly was my baby brother born?'

'He isn't your baby brother, Raul.' All the sympathy she'd felt for him as she'd read the contents of the envelope rushed back at her and she looked into his handsome face, watching the colour drain away beneath the olive tones of his skin.

Raul merely looked at her, the shock on his face clear.

'He is older than you, Raul.' She could still feel the pain his mother must have felt, the hard underlining in black pen of Max's birth date giving away so much. 'That is probably why your father set this whole thing up. To ensure you find his heir.'

'How much older?' Shock echoed in Raul's voice. 'Four months.'

She had been so stunned by it all, by the revelations that Raul maybe wasn't the heir to his father's fortune, she hadn't been able to tell him. She'd spent the last few days checking it all out and now she knew for sure that footballer legend turned entrepreneur after a bad car accident, Maximiliano Martinez, was his brother. Two powerful and wealthy men. It was going to be some showdown when they met.

Raul pulled her closer and she gasped, the sudden movement in complete contrast to the anger shining brightly in his eyes, but she moulded herself against him, the attraction she felt too strong to ignore, as was the need to salve his obvious pain.

'What are you doing?' The words flew spontaneously from her when his hand pressed against her lower back, forcing her so close it was almost intimate—too intimate.

'Dancing with you.'

She wanted that more than anything else right now, but deep down she didn't trust herself. The intimate way he held her, the deep, desire-filled look in his eyes lured her and she couldn't allow it to happen even though she wanted it—wanted him.

He lowered his head and whispered in her ear. 'Carlos is watching us closely. I want him to see desire, show them that the deal our fathers struck has not defeated me—or you.'

She looked up at him as her heart thudded. 'Desire?' The word was barely audible as his face came so close to hers that it would be easy to tilt her chin up and kiss him. Just as she had done once before.

'Yes, Lydia, desire. Can you do that? Then we can leave, get away from all this deceit.'

'What about your plans to show we are happily engaged?' Her words were a husky whisper and, despite all her reservations, she knew the same desire that had taken over that night in the rain was pushing her on now, turning her into a different woman.

'Right now I want them to think we are so consumed by one another that we have to leave.'

Her heart went out to him. He needed to leave in order to deal with all she'd just told him. How did it feel to discover you were not your father's first-born as you'd always believed? No wonder his father had attached such a bizarre condition to the will. He wanted his firstborn to inherit equally and had done everything in his power to ensure it happened.

Consumed by desire and sympathy, she reached up, placed her palm against his face, feeling the new growth of stubble. Her gaze became riveted to his, seeing the passion building with them. Compassion fused with passion and her attention moved to his lips, remembering the electric kiss in the rain. Had it been the sudden downpour that had made that kiss so intense, so memorable? Or the man himself?

As the questions raced through her mind and the desire to lean closer grew ever stronger, she tried to fight it. Raul didn't. With a fierce intensity his lips claimed hers, sending her mind reeling and her heart thumping and the power of that contact shot through her entire body, unlocking an unbearable need deep within her.

Silently she gave thanks that they were in the middle of a dance floor, that all around them people could surely see the fire that had sparked to life. But she wanted more and to her horror she wished they weren't at the party, wished that they were alone and able to follow the heady trail of passion to its ultimate conclusion.

Raul pulled back from her, his eyes darker than she'd ever seen them. 'I'm taking you home. Right now—and then I'm going to make love to you.'

No. That was the word she wanted to say, the word she should say, but for a moment it wouldn't come and when it did it was a breathy whisper. 'No, we can't. That's not part of the deal.'

'To hell with the deal.'

'Raul,' she pleaded even though inside her body clamoured with excitement and need for this man.

He brushed his lips so lightly over hers she almost sighed with pleasure. 'Tonight you will be mine, Lydia.'

She had to remember what this was all about, but did the deal really matter any more? Hadn't she done her part? She'd found his brother, her dues were paid, her father's debt now clear. So where did that leave her now?

Could she walk away from this moment, this man? He'd got to her, entered her mind, her thoughts, her very soul and, even though she knew she shouldn't, she wanted him, wanted to be his, to feel the passion and desire so completely.

Her heart was leading her head, her desire for him all-consuming. 'Take me home, Raul.'

CHAPTER SEVEN

LYDIA'S HEART THUMPED and her body hummed with anticipation as Raul's car stopped outside his apartment. There was no mistaking the intent in Raul's eyes, just as she couldn't deny the need within her. A need that had boiled up rapidly, blending together with the shock that she'd been so bold, creating an intoxicating cocktail that couldn't be denied—by either of them. It was strong and powerful. The kind of attraction that, if she was honest, had sealed her fate the day they had first met.

His eyes said all that needed to be said as he got out of the car, took her hand and she stepped out into the crisp evening air. In one hungry sweep his gaze devoured her, ratcheting up the tension, the anticipation, smothering the nerves and apprehension over what she was about to do, making her want him, want this night more than ever.

He still held her hand, the heat of his touch scorching her, and without a word he led her into the building, calling the elevator. Was he still angry at what she'd told him about Max? Or was it her use of Spanish? Had he put everything but what they were about to do from his mind? Was he so focused on desire that he thought of nothing else? Could she really affect him like that?

'Raul?' His name slipped out as a question, her eyes searching his firmly set profile as the elevator took them up to his apartment. The tension in the confines of the mirrored walls all but exploded as his gaze met hers, the unconcealed desire in his eyes echoing around her from the reflective surfaces.

Hungry need met innocent desire, becoming something else, something she couldn't deny even if she wanted to. There would be no turning back now. This strong, powerful man was what she needed, even if it was for one night only.

'You have found Max so are no longer bound by our agreement.' The sharpness of his words was in total contrast to the desire burning in his eyes, making the dark depths unreadable.

'I'm not?'

'You have done what you promised, Lydia. You are free to go back to London.' There was a hint of warning in his voice, warning she had no intention of heeding.

'And if I don't want to?' Her heart went into free fall at her boldness, the likes of which she'd never known before. How could one man change her so much? 'Not yet anyway.'

She couldn't believe how shameless she sounded and knew it came from something much deeper than just passion. All she wanted now was to stay, to discover more with this man even though she'd constantly fought him and the attraction that had leapt to life between them. But why, when such an action went against everything she believed in? When he'd been the man who'd humiliated her as a sixteen-year-old?

Because you've seen beneath the tough exterior, seen who he really is.

He stopped abruptly and looked at her, the intensity in his eyes so wild, so very daring she could scarcely breathe as the elevator doors opened onto the opulent space of his apartment. 'You should only walk through these doors with me if you want me to kiss you.'

'I want that.' She searched his face, looking for the man she had glimpsed, the man who hid behind the toughened exterior of billionaire businessman Raul Valdez. 'I want you to kiss me, Raul, like you did the other night—in the rain.'

He reached out to her, his thumb and finger lifting her chin a fraction, the heat of his touch almost too much as she swallowed back the nerves that threatened once more. Just as she thought she couldn't look into his eyes any longer he moved closer, his lips so very close she could feel his breath, warm on her face.

'If I kiss you again, Lydia, it will become far more than that. I don't want a shy innocent in my bed. I want the passionate woman I know you are, the one you have kept hidden from me.'

Did he really think that of her? She drew in a breath as a rush of panic skittered over her. She might not be a virgin, but she was still innocent to the ways of a man like Raul. She had only known one other man, her ex-fiancé.

'I want to be that woman again, but this time I want more than a kiss. Much more.' She blushed at the thought, trying to put aside his obvious dislike for a woman who had very little experience of sex. She would have to continue the act of confidence and sophistication if she wanted to experience a night with this man—and she did. 'Tonight is for us, Raul.'

In answer he brushed his lips provocatively over hers, sending a rush of heady desire round her until it unlocked the passion she'd been fighting since that first meeting in London.

Desperate to hide her inexperience, she pressed herself against his body, the answering groan as he deepened the kiss setting light to her desire again. With her hands behind his neck, her fingers in the dark hair at his collar, she pulled him to her, her tongue slipping boldly into his mouth, teasing in a way she'd had no idea she knew how to do. Raul Valdez had turned her into a very different woman.

With a swiftness that had her gasping in shock,

he pulled away from her and, taking her hand in his, strode purposefully to his apartment, unaware she struggled to keep up in the heels she'd teamed with her dress.

He pushed open the door and, with a wild look in his eyes, pulled her towards him, slamming the door shut as he did so. Before she could blink, his lean hard body pressed her against the door and any doubt she had that he wanted her no longer existed. The fire of need leapt to life as he pressed himself intimately against her.

What are you doing?

The sane and sensible Lydia surfaced once more and she looked into his brooding eyes, the feral darkness almost intimidating. She pressed her palm against his chest, exerting pressure, but he didn't yield. Instead his lips came down on hers with such force her knees buckled and only the solid door and his firm body kept her upright. It was a plundering and ruthless kiss, one that swiped the sensible Lydia out of the room, and as his hands slid up her waist to her breast she knew that version of herself wouldn't come back tonight—and she didn't want her to.

Raul's hand cupped her breast and the fire of need within him raged ever higher. He must be going mad. To want a woman so much, but now it was too late. Part of him had wanted her to stop him, to act the high and mighty woman he'd first met in London and coldly rebuff him. The innocent girl she'd been all those years ago when they'd first met had been replaced by a sassy and very sexy woman. One who made it clear she wanted him as much as he wanted her.

She'd encouraged him, drawn him deeper into this madness when they had arrived at his apartment, the change in her, the lack of resistance all too clear. Was it because she now knew she was free of him, that the threat of marriage, which had at first seemed the only way to clear her father's debts, was now over?

Whatever it was, he was incapable of rational thought at this moment and he intended to take all she offered—and more. He intended to lose himself in passion, to drown in desire, because right now it was the only way to block out the hurt that had been lurking in the shadows of his life for as long as he could remember. Hurt he had no control over, but passion he did.

'This has to go.' His words were as feral as his desire and he pulled at the strap of her dress, but it didn't yield.

'So impatient.' Lydia's husky voice, full of flirtation, threatened to push him over the edge. She wriggled against him as she tried to reach behind her and unfasten the dress.

'Allow me.' He fought to calm his wayward body as he stepped back from her, placed his hands on her arms and gently began to turn her.

Her gaze met his for a split second before she willingly turned her back to him. He looked at the creamy soft skin, the sexy shape of her spine, and cursed the thin strap across her shoulder blades that had held the dress in place. Perhaps it was just as well the dress hadn't been discarded in an instant because now he had a tighter rein on the desire she ignited within him. He watched as she breathed in, deeply and evenly, then slowly he unclipped the thin silver strap.

'There's another at my waist.' Her voice was a husky whisper. She didn't move but the sexual chemistry between them was building, getting stronger with each breath she took. The air around them so charged with fire and passion that if he struck a match they'd go up in flames.

He didn't say a word as he traced his fingers down her spine, smiling with satisfaction when she arched slightly beneath his light touch. She lowered her head forwards, her hair slipping away from her neck, and all he could think about was trailing his lips against the soft skin there and down her back.

Instead he focused his attention on unfastening the dress, which had clung to her slender hips, sparkling invitingly all evening, daring him to want her. Slowly he slid his hands up her bare back, pushing his fingers beneath the straps at her shoulders, then as if in slow motion he watched the straps slide down her arms where they stopped in the bends of her elbows, preventing him from seeing her gloriously naked.

With a stab of shock, he realised she stood with her palms flat against the door of his apartment, her head lowered, her breathing deep and rapid with desire. When had he ever wanted a woman so much he hadn't been able to get further than the front door? Never. He hadn't ever wanted to claim a woman as his with the urgency that flooded him now. What was so different about this woman?

He should lead her to the bedroom before they went any further, but even as the thought flitted through his mind he dismissed it. Before he could stop himself he had moved closer to her, his hands going inside the heavy sequined material that hung loosely from her. He slipped his arms around her waist, pulling her against him and smoothing his palms over her stomach, then her ribs and then up to her breasts. The scent of her perfume, seductive rose and jasmine, only served to notch up the tension even further, heightening his need for her.

He kissed her neck and she sighed softly, but as his fingers teased her nipples the sound became distinctly more untamed. 'We should take this to the bedroom, should we not, *querida*?'

He could feel every deep and erratic breath she took as his hands caressed her breasts. Still her hands were pressed flat against his door, but the whole sensation was so different, so erotic, he could stay like this, enjoying the mounting desire, for far longer than if she were now completely naked on his bed.

'Yes.' That one word was so loaded with sexual tension he nearly groaned aloud, then she looked back at him, her green eyes so dark they resembled the depths of the forest, hidden from the sun. 'We should.'

She turned to him; the dress that had been so seductively tight over her breasts now lingered alluringly on her arms, tempting him, and he bit down on the wild desire to all but rip the silver fabric from her.

'This way, *querida*.' He held out his hand to her, giving her one last chance to back away, one last chance to stop the madness of the desire that was flowing like a raging river between them.

She didn't falter as she took his hand, and as they walked towards his bedroom her heels tapped on the hard floor. Each step she took was firm and decisive. She wanted this as much as he did.

The urge to rush, to take her swiftly and make her his had subsided, in its place a need to be calm, gentle. That way he could lose himself in desire, forget the world beyond whilst he savoured every moment of the night with Lydia, determined to wipe out all she meant, all she was connected to. He wanted to forget who she really was for one night. Somewhere in the recesses of his mind he knew she was different, knew this was a glimpse of the kind of life, the sort of love he could have had if his past hadn't shaped him into a hard and emotionless man.

This was the kind of woman a man could love, the kind of woman *he* could love if he allowed himself to. But that would never happen. Love was a weakness and he would never be weak.

Lydia stood in his room, the large opulent bed dominating the space, competing with the man whose hand she had taken willingly as she'd walked with him towards this moment. She should have turned and run, as far as she could, when he'd given her the chance—and he'd given enough of them. She hadn't because she wanted this too much, wanted him, wanted this one night.

'Turn around.' The firmness of his voice was tempered by the husky desire lingering in it. She did as she was told for no other reason than she wanted to. She wanted to go back to the moment of minutes ago when she could feel his touch, his breath warm on her neck as he'd kissed her, his body, firm and hard against hers; she wanted to believe this was something special, something more than the one night it so obviously was.

She shuddered as he placed his hands on her shoulders, sliding down her arms and taking the dress with them. The air was cool on her naked breasts as the dress slithered down over her hips and to the floor. Then, just as he had done before, his fingers trailed fire down her spine, pausing to make circles of pleasure on her skin as they reached the thin straps of her thong.

'Very sexy.' A feral depth had entered his voice and she couldn't help but smile. He certainly knew how to make a woman feel attractive and desired. Something she definitely wasn't used to.

Emboldened by the heady desire that coursed through her, she turned, scarcely giving a thought to the dress at her feet. All she wanted was to meet his passion, to lose herself in the moment.

She reached out to tug at his bow tie, pulling it slowly whilst looking directly into his eyes. 'I'm feeling a little underdressed at the moment.'

His brows rose in amusement, but his voice had become a hoarse whisper. 'I disagree, *querida*. Stilettos and those sexy panties are perfect.'

She let his tie drop against his white shirt as she moved closer, his arms pulling her against him, the soft fabric of his jacket brushing against her bare breasts. Just when she thought she couldn't stand it any longer he lowered his head; slowly and very seductively he brushed his lips over hers. Her arms wound around his neck as a soft sigh of pleasure slipped from her, only to be stolen by his lips as he deepened the kiss, giving into the fierce need that enveloped them.

With purpose he moved against her, pushing her back towards the big bed, but as her legs met it her knees buckled and she tumbled back, bringing him with her. His weight pressed her into the soft covers, the hardness of his arousal pressing insistently against her thighs, sending her desire to new heights.

'I want you, Raul.'

He looked down at her, his eyes so dark it was like looking at the velvety midnight sky and so easy to brush aside what this really was, so easy to fool herself into believing it was so much more.

He levered himself off her, looking so sexy, so handsome she wondered if she was dreaming, but the huskiness of his voice left her in no doubt that this was real.

'Nothing would give me more pleasure.' He smiled, a lazy and intoxicating smile, as he shrugged off his jacket, opened his shirt, button by button in such a teasing way she bit down hard on her lower lip as the anticipation of being his, being made love to by this virile specimen of masculinity, rushed over her.

Each breath she took as she watched him until he was completely naked was harder than the next. Her heart pounded wildly as he crossed the room with little regard for the fact that he was proudly erect. She watched as, with a hint of a smile, he opened a drawer next to the bed and took out the all-important contraception, placing the packet next to the lamp.

'For our protection, *querida*.'

How had she not even questioned that? Had he

blinded her so much with desire that she'd given no thought to such necessities? She blushed as his smile widened then he moved back onto the bed, covering her completely, and the heat of his erection, with only the barrier of her skimpy panties, as it pressed against her made her gasp with pleasure.

It had never felt like this before.

'Tonight you are mine.' Raul's whispered words as he kissed her neck, his hands expertly making her body burn with fiery need, made anything else but the ultimate conclusion impossible.

His fingers hooked into the strings of her panties and she gasped as he pulled. The sound of ripping stitches as erotic as the expression on his handsome face.

'Don't forget the condom.' Her words held a hint of panic that she hoped he wouldn't notice. Now was not the time to enlighten him to the fact that she was far from experienced in the art of lovemaking, so much so she hadn't given a thought to contraception as desire had whisked her away.

He kissed her lips then looked down at her. 'Patience, *querida*. Patience.'

Then before she could say anything else his hand slid from her hip to the heated centre of her desire and she raised herself up as his touch brought a sensation she'd never known washing over her. As the torment continued she was aware of him speaking, aware of the Spanish words, but had no idea what he was saying, only that it increased the desire to dizzying heights.

In one swift move he rolled away from her, leaving her trembling in the wake of the pleasure that had just happened. She opened her eyes and looked at him. Would he have known that was the first time she'd ever known such pleasure?

He looked at her as he opened the packet, the intensity in his eyes making them so very dark. With a suggestive raise of his brows he rolled on the condom, then before she even had time to blush his body was overs her, his long lean legs pushing hers apart. Without any encouragement other than the constant hum of desire within her, she lifted her legs, wrapping them around him, lifting herself up to his possession.

With wild words in Spanish, so guttural she couldn't make them out, he thrust into her, making her gasp and press her fingernails into his back. The erratic thumping of desire exploded wildly inside her as she moved with him, taking him deeper as he claimed her, harder and faster. It was explosive, wild, but completely wonderful.

'I never thought...' she gasped as she clung to him, the waves of passion crashing harder and faster over her, making her thoughts as disjointed as her words '...it could be like this...'

He silenced her with kisses as they moved together until the world splintered and she floated above the earth, barely conscious of his wild desire-induced growl.

'Don't think,' Raul said between deep and hard breaths. 'Tonight I will not allow you to think, not when such passion, such fiery desire still hums between us.'

'It does?' Her voice trembled as he slid away from her, her body cooling, and she was able to focus once more.

His lips hovered over hers, his breath hot as he teased her. She closed her eyes, wanting his kiss and so much more. When it came the kiss was hard and demanding but he pulled back enough to look at her and she opened her eyes, trying to hide the need, the disappointment that it was over.

'It does, *querida*, and we have the whole night ahead of us.'

'All night,' she replied in Spanish, kissing him and allowing all her hungry desire to show.

CHAPTER EIGHT

THE WHISPERS OF a new day had begun to slip into the room as Lydia opened her eyes, acutely aware of the warmth of Raul's body against hers. It also confirmed to her questioning mind that last night had really happened. The exquisite passion hadn't been the dreams of a woman falling harder and harder for a man who'd coldly told her love was for fools.

Last night had been very real, deepening her feelings to newer levels, but now what should she do? Should she slip from the bed and return to her room? Slowly she moved, pushing aside the covers very carefully. She looked at Raul's watch, lying on the bedside table after it had been discarded last night. It was still early and as she watched the seconds ticking away the thump of her heart became louder.

'You are not going anywhere, *querida*.' Raul's voice, heavy with sleep, instantly stilled her then his arm wrapped around her waist, pulling her naked body back into bed and against his. He might still be in the clutches of sleep, but he wanted her, she was in no doubt of that.

'Now that is such a tempting idea.' She turned in his arms, trying to fight the rising desire in her, wanting to sound carefree and flirtatious, as if this were a situation she was used to. Last night she'd wanted him to think she was an experienced lover and now she wanted him to think she knew exactly how it went—the etiquette of waking up beside a man who had been your lover for one night only.

'The night isn't over yet.' His husky voice sent a tingle all over her as his hands slid down her body to her hips, where his fingers lightly circled on her skin, teasing her until she knew she wasn't going to be able to resist him.

She laughed brightly, fighting the urge to give into the heady desire now burning brightly within her once more. 'It's almost morning.'

'Don't tease me with your sexy body.' The Spanish words were soft and seductive as he brushed his lips against hers and she closed her eyes, imagining the kiss was because he loved her, because they were something more than one-night lovers.

She pushed against his chest with her palms, ignoring the firm muscle beneath her fingers, the soft hair she just wanted to run her hands through. Inwardly she groaned with a mixture of despair and longing, outwardly she laughed again.

'I am not a tease, Raul Valdez.' Her voice was so light, so playful it didn't even sound like her.

'You are,' he began as his hand moved up her waist to cover the firmness of her breast, making her drag in a deep breath as passion exploded inside her. 'And very sexy.'

'Sexy?' she questioned coyly, not able to believe she was being so flirtatious. Was it because she didn't want the night to end, didn't want the daylight to bring the harsh reality of having become just another one of his conquests?

He pulled her closer, his intentions emblazoned in the black depths of his eyes. Her heart raced as she surrendered to his kiss, to his caress. She wanted this so much—wanted him. She put her heart and soul into the kiss, allowing it to convey all the emotions she could never tell him.

'*Sí, querida*. Very sexy.' He whispered the words against her lips, the sensation wildly erotic. 'And now I can't let you go.'

'Is that so?' She moved daringly against him, enjoying the momentary rush of power, but not for one minute did she believe she was truly in control. That kind of mistake could be fatal with a man like Raul Valdez.

In a movement so swift she gasped, Raul pushed her back against the softness of the pillow, the weight of his naked body preventing her escape. Laughter glittered in his eyes as he looked into hers and she

wanted to hang on to this moment for ever, to remember how it felt to be loved by him and to love
him in return.

'You are not going anywhere, not until I have
made love to you again and again.' His voice had
become deep and husky, adding to the fire of desire
that was rapidly burning out of control within her.

'But it's nearly morning.'

'Then we shall have all day, no, all weekend together.'

'All weekend?' Now she was shocked. Was he
saying it as some kind of test for her? After all,
hadn't she insisted on being his for just one night?

'Yes. One weekend of passion and I don't intend
to waste a moment more of it.'

Before she could respond, offer up any kind of defence, his lips were claiming hers in a hot kiss, the
heat of his body coaxing hers into submission and
she knew she couldn't fight it any longer.

It had been hard to leave Lydia in bed, but as the mid-
morning winter sunshine streamed into his apartment Raul had done just that. Their lovemaking had
been powerful and passionate, but as Lydia had slept
his thoughts had wandered. Now she was sitting opposite him as they had breakfast, the air of aloofness
she often hid behind threatening to return. But he
wasn't ready to end it yet.

'I thought you wanted to go to London today.'

Lydia's voice held a note of uncertainty and he downed a black coffee in one go, needing the hit of caffeine to calm him. After last night's revelations— all of them—there was no way he was going to step out of this erotic interlude and into his future. For now, that could all wait. He still wanted Lydia with a burning need that made him want to drag her straight back to bed and it was the perfect defence against acknowledging the truth.

Was it her obvious innocence last night, before she'd become a bold and flirtatious lover, or a way of punishing her for being the one who'd changed his life? He didn't know. Either way, he wanted her. He wasn't about to turn his back on such an alluring companion. Not yet. She would be his for the week-end. On Monday he would return to reality and fly to London to meet his brother. Once he'd done that, Lydia would be free—he would be free. Their lives could return to normal.

Except that his never would. His would change be-yond recognition. He had a brother. One he wanted to know, and it had nothing to do with money as Lydia had accused him of.

He and his brother shared the misfortune of hav-ing the same father. Didn't that count for something? He frowned as he thought of Carlos's insistence that he marry instead of looking for Max. Was that really to ensure Lydia's father didn't get away without re-paying his debt or was Carlos reluctant to have two

Valdez sons at the helm of the company? Was it possible there was something else going on?

'Would you rather I walked out so soon after last night?' He dragged his mind back to the present and glared at Lydia, unable to keep the annoyance from his voice that she could so easily move on from all they'd shared last night.

'But last night, you said you would be going today.'

'That was before our lovers' tryst.' He watched the glow of a blush rush over her cheeks and, even though anger was the best emotion to deal with what was to come, he smiled. 'I am not in the habit of making love to a woman and then running off into the night. We will spend the weekend together. Like lovers. Then we will go to London on Monday.'

'You want me to come with you?' She sat opposite him, her silk dressing gown doing little to hide the fact that beneath it she was naked, and he gritted his teeth against the sudden stab of lust that shot through him.

Slowly he put down his cup, then stood up and put out his hand to her. With a guarded expression in her eyes she took his hand and he pulled her to her feet, then with his free hand tugged at the belt tied loosely at her waist. The cream silk slipped apart, exposing her to his hungry gaze.

'I want nothing more than to make love to you again and again. This weekend is for us. The future can damn well wait.'

He shoved aside the agony of having that cruel confirmation that his father had never really wanted him, never really cared for him in any way. Now he knew why he'd had to put up with such a harsh up-bringing, why anything he'd done had never pleased his father.

His father had never wanted him. He hadn't been the much-sought-after son and heir. That honour had fallen to Max, the son who'd taken his name, the name he should have had, just months before he'd been born. How could he ever have competed with that? Did he want to? The question lingered in his mind.

And this woman had known that cruel fact since they'd visited his mother and had kept it from him. He bit down on the anger and allowed desire to flow through him. He needed it to forget the pain. Passion and desire made very good salves for such wounds.

'We should go out, take a walk in the park or something.' There was hesitancy in her voice, which only increased his suspicion that she was far from the experienced lover she wanted him to believe her to be. Even her teasing this morning hadn't completely disguised the fact. He'd seen something in her eyes, something deep and meaningful.

Very well. He would play the part of lover and forget the real world that awaited him.

'We can.' He pulled her closer, feeling the heat of her body scorch his. 'After I've explored your sexy body, kissed every part of it and made you cry out my name as you did early this morning.'

She blushed prettily and he kissed her, tempting her, feeling her resistance subsiding. Whatever else happened, she was his for now. But it couldn't last. He'd never wanted sentiments and emotions in his life and, despite the new and powerful draw to her, Lydia wasn't going to change that.

Lydia lay languidly in bed as darkness fell over Madrid, the apartment becoming the romantic place it had been last night, lit with only a few lamps. They had left the apartment to stroll around the cafés and bars in Madrid's plaza. But the undercurrent of sexual attraction meant that neither of them had had much appetite for food. As the winter sun had given way to the night, they'd returned to the warmth of the apartment and Lydia was hardly able to believe they were still in a lovers' limbo. She should be happy, should just enjoy it for what it was, but foolishly she wanted more—and knew it was impossible.

She'd never known such pleasure existed. Raul had shown her that lovemaking was something wonderful but she knew it wasn't lovemaking to him. It was merely lust—overwhelming desire and passion.

The sound of Raul in the shower dragged her from dwelling too much on what could never be. For Raul she knew this whole weekend was based on desire and lust. It was more than lust for her. Could it be possible that she'd fallen for him—really fallen for him? Or was it that she still felt sorry for him, still felt the pain and vulnerability she'd seen in his eyes when she'd told him about Max? As he'd looked at her, the party going on around them, all she'd wanted was to ease that pain, to be the one to make things right for him.

This morning his lovemaking had been wild and hard, the gentle dominance of last night had turned to something more determined and Lydia had found it as exciting as their first passionate encounter. Finally, that anger had dissipated and the man who'd driven her mad with desire, making her throw caution aside and be his for the night, had returned.

She'd been bold, flirtatiously asking for more than sex, asking for something that resembled a real relationship, even though it would be only for two days. To her astonishment he had agreed and she had enjoyed his company over lunch. Had he enjoyed the day as much as her? Had he liked being a couple? And what happened now?

'Should we go out this evening?' She slipped from the bed and pulled on the silk dressing gown as he returned from the shower, a white towel around his hips, his hair dark with wetness. She couldn't take her eyes from him, he looked so sexy, so handsome.

'I think our absence from this evening's party will say so much more than our attendance.' The deep sultry tone of her voice made smiling coyly at him the only option, but deep down the worry still lingered that he was using her to prove something, to further his dealings with his board.

'What did you have planned, then?' She couldn't believe she, of all people, was being so teasing and behaving like a seductress.

'Other than to make love to the most beautiful English rose?' He moved towards her and she shivered in anticipation.

'Yes, other than that.' With a flaunting smile she stepped past him. 'I'd like to talk a little, get to know you better.'

He tensed, the muscles of his chest flexing, proving if nothing else that this weekend was only about sex. She turned her attention to knotting the belt in her dressing gown, desperate to hide her disappointment from him and, even more importantly, not question it herself.

'Very well. We shall eat here and talk over a glass of wine.'

She frowned at him, wondering what it was he had planned now, because if there was one thing she'd learnt about him it was that he always had plans. Whatever those plans were she was determined to drive the conversation the way she wanted, to find out just what the future held for her and her family. Was she really clear of debt? The one question she wouldn't ask was what the future held for them—as a couple.

'What are you going to do—about Max?' The question slipped from her as she lay in bed, casually trailing a finger across the fine cotton sheets.

He looked at her as he tossed aside the towel and put his clothes on, the blue shirt only highlighting the jet black of his hair. He was avoiding answering her. Was he hoping he could rid himself of Max in the same way he intended to rid himself of her?

He stood tall and proud, defiance coming off him in waves, and she knew without any doubt that it was most certainly not what he wanted. 'I will welcome Max into my life and the family business.'

'Because of loyalty to your father?' She pulled the sheet against her. Such a discussion needed modesty.

'No.' He finished dressing and looked at her, his gaze sweeping over her, and her skin burned as if she were completely naked to his gaze. There was desire in his eyes, but also something else, something unfathomable, something very cold. 'Out of necessity.'

The barb of his statement hit her hard and although it was powerful it at least confirmed that she and the man she'd become temporarily engaged to would soon go their separate ways. It was exactly the deal she'd made with herself as she'd given in to the temptation of desire and had truly become his lover.

'The lesser of two evils?' She taunted him, needing to counteract the pain she felt. Pain that came

from feeling deeply for this man—far too deeply.
'Either welcome a brother or a wife.'

'*Sí, querida.* To prove I am not the heartless man
my father assumed I was. He thought I'd find marriage preferable to bringing my brother into my life.'

Was he running from the truth now as she was?
And what was his truth? With a heavy heart she
knew it would not be that he had fallen in love with
her, that he wanted more than this passionate weekend. She realised she was decidedly underdressed
and vulnerability shivered over her as once again
his gaze lingered on her.

'So I am free to go?' She dared to ask, dared to
bring their lovers' weekend crashing down around
her.

His brows rose and he crossed the room towards
her, his height dominating the entire room, and even
though she was covered only in a sheet she looked
defiantly back at him. He sat on the bed next to her,
reached out and stroked the backs of his fingers
across her cheek in a moment so tender, so out of
place, she had to blink back the urge to cry.

'But you don't want to go now, do you, *querida*?
Not when the passion still burns so hotly between
us. You want to stay, to sleep in my bed and be the
woman I desire.'

His seductive words stoked the slumbering fire
of desire to life once more and she knew she was
lost, that whatever she'd promised herself about not
falling for him, she would never be able to keep it.

'What I want is for you to come back to bed,' she teased as she smiled up at him.

He moved towards her, his kiss so light, so very loving she could almost believe it was real. 'How can I resist such a seductress?'

CHAPTER NINE

THE PASSION THAT had ignited between them as they'd danced at the party two nights ago still flowed through Raul. A concept he was far from familiar with and, even though he wanted Lydia, he'd suggested they take a walk, as most people in Madrid did on a Sunday afternoon. She looked as if she belonged here, strolling with the locals, her long legs encased in white jeans and boots, the collar of her black faux suede jacket fanning out her hair around her. He had to do something to cool things down.

Tomorrow he would be stepping out of this strangeness he'd fallen into and back into his real life. He'd be in London to meet his brother. A thought that brought happiness and annoyance in equal measures.

'Have you spoken to your father?' he asked and her step faltered beside him as they entered Retiro Park; the trees bare of leaves but bathed in the winter sun, it still looked inviting. He'd spent many hours here, first as a young boy and then a man. Sometimes he'd had the company of a woman, but it had never been to avoid the lure of taking one to his bed yet again.

'No. That is a conversation for another day. What about you? Have you said anything to your mother yet?' He glanced at her as she successfully turned the tables on him and a spark of admiration shot through him. Lydia was more than a match for him. He liked that. Not that it changed a thing. Tomorrow it would end. It was what they'd planned—what they wanted.

'I think it will be better to tell her when I have met my brother, seen what kind of man he is. I insist on protecting her from this as much as possible.' As he spoke she took his arm and moved closer to him and to the outside world they looked no different from any other couple in love strolling through the park.

It wasn't what he wanted. Love and other such ill-fated emotions weakened even the strongest man and, combined with the desire he had for Lydia, Raul sensed that it would be all-consuming—and lethal. No, it was not something he wanted or needed in his life.

'I admire that in you.' She spoke softly and he looked down at her, to see she was watching him. The distance he was hoping to create between them slipped away as she smiled, openly and honestly. Hell, he wanted to kiss her.

A fierce fire leapt to life within him, filling his whole body with something he didn't want, some-thing he couldn't deal with. He'd known desire before, many times, but never like this. Could it be he'd crossed the boundary and was straying into a place he had no intention of being?

He focused his mind on the conversation, ignoring the undertones of something much more devastating. 'That I care for my mother? The woman who raised me, protecting me from the true knowledge of my father's secret life?'

Saying it aloud to Lydia brought it all home to him. How much his mother must have suffered because of the man she'd married, not out of love, but out of duty and honour to her family.

He saw it all differently. He could hear again Lydia proudly telling him she had no intention of marrying him. All it did was back up the relief that she'd fulfilled her part of the deal and had found Max, unlocking the funds to clear the debt, funds that he strongly suspected his father had thought would never be unlocked.

'But that is not wrong, Raul.' She looked at him, a strange and powerful expression in her lovely green eyes. If he didn't know how fiercely she opposed the idea of marriage and how she agreed on his philosophy of love, he could be fooled into thinking she was in love. With him.

'Wrong or not, it is not up for discussion.' He held her gaze for a second longer, then turned to walk on. They were drawing attention, he realised. 'Let us walk.'

She fell quickly into step beside him, her black

boots making a gentle sound on the path, and feeling her body against his as they walked felt so right, so natural. For the briefest of moments, he wondered why he didn't want this closeness, this total commitment.

Because it will never last and pain will follow it.

He could still clearly remember just what such pain had done to his mother when she'd discovered his father had led a secret life. It was the kind of pain that went hand in hand with that elusive emotion love and it had convinced him that, despite all his mother had claimed about their marriage being arranged, she'd loved his father.

He would never be that weak. He would never open himself up to such pain.

'The park is beautiful at this time of the year, is it not?' He diverted his thoughts and the topic of conversation onto more neutral territory.

'It is, even when it is so cold.' She snuggled against him. Was she cold or getting too comfortable? 'It's lovely, thanks.'

'A nice way to end our weekend, no?' He felt her glance up at him, but he kept his attention firmly ahead. Was it possible she was reading more into this moment?

'Yes,' she said and walked on, looking anywhere but at him, convincing him he must have been mistaken. At least she agreed and there wouldn't be any drama when they returned to their lives. This would be just a weekend affair.

* * *

Lydia breathed in the cold air, relishing the gentle breeze on her face as she walked, her arm linked in Raul's, through Retiro Park. The soft luxury of his camel cashmere coat was warm and inviting, but not nearly as much as Raul. The wind was cold, but it focused her thoughts, stopped her from believing this affair would ever be anything more than just a weekend. One that was almost over. It had been a magical interlude, which had shown her what loving a man could be like, even though she knew this man would never allow anyone close enough to love him or to love himself.

'We will go to London tomorrow.' As if he'd sensed her thoughts, taken lead from them, Raul said the words that spelt the end of whatever it was that had happened between them since the night of the party.

'So this is goodbye?' She kept walking, looking ahead of her down the long tree-lined path, noticing the red squirrels that cheekily followed them from tree to tree in the hope of treats. Normally she would have remarked upon it, taken pleasure in such a moment, but not today—not now. She wanted to be as detached as he was, her words as emotionless and empty and, whilst she was happy that she'd achieved that, inside she was breaking apart.

'Sí, querida.' His Spanish accent was deeper than ever and the use of the now all too familiar term of endearment no longer irritated. She glanced up at him, his profile strong and unyielding. 'It is time to return to our lives.'

She should be elated. Her father's debts were to be cleared without the need to enter into a marriage more in keeping with the kind of historical novels she'd loved as a teenager. Tomorrow she would return to London and she and Raul would never have to see one another again. So why did that feel so difficult? As foolish as it was, she had fallen in love with a man who was as cold and incapable of love as his father had evidently been.

'I will of course require written proof that my father's debts are settled. I don't want to be hounded again.' The pain of her realisation made her lash out, made her want to hurt him too. But could you ever hurt a man so incapable of emotions?

'Hounded?' He pulled her to a halt and looked down at her, the spark of anger once again in his eyes. Inwardly she sighed. It seemed she brought out the worst in this man.

She lifted her chin defiantly; the barrier she usually hid behind, the one she had lowered over the last few days, slid perfectly back into place. He would never know her true feelings for him. Never. 'Yes, hounded.'

He narrowed his eyes, their dark depths searching her face. 'In that case, after tomorrow's meeting with my brother, you will be pleased to know I will have no further cause to *hound* you, as you so nicely put it. Our engagement will be over.'

'Then you should have this back.' She pulled her arm free of his, the comfortable companionship of moments ago gone for good. It was for the best and, trying to push down the pain, she slid the engagement ring from her finger. 'I have no need of it any longer.'

The expression on his face held a hint of that amusement she found so annoying but, even so, a twinge of regret raced through her. The last few days had been so different, the pressure to be anything but herself had disappeared and she'd felt more comfortable with him than she had with anyone. The thought of giving it up saddened her. Was what they'd shared over the last few days what being in a real relationship felt like? Was that the closest she would ever come to knowing love?

'And I do?' The imperious question held such command that the birds in the trees above them seemed to stop singing, as if waiting to see what would happen next.

'Next time you need a convenient fiancée you will have the ring ready and at your disposal.' All the hurt she'd felt echoed in her words, despite her trying to keep it in.

His eyes darkened with anger and with a satisfied smile she turned and began to walk once more. It took seconds for him to join her.

'I had thought you were different.'

'From what?' She kept her voice light and flirtatious, determined he shouldn't guess at the hurt that was lancing through her, the broken and unattainable dreams this weekend had brought to light.

'From the spoilt little rich girl I first met at the dinner party. From the demanding woman who'd waited for me in the restaurant three weeks ago.' The silky softness of his voice almost disguised the underlying disgust at just who he thought she really was.

'Maybe that was part of the act.' She didn't look at him. She didn't dare. She focused on the long path ahead of them, trying instead to wonder what the other people walking in the park were doing. Wondering if they were happy and in love as she'd almost begun to believe she might be. What a fool she'd been.

The night of the dinner party, when she'd first met Raul, she'd acted to a role she'd thought her father had wanted her to play. It had been one last futile attempt at bridging the ever growing gap between her and her father. It had also been what had made Raul look at her with distaste. From that moment onwards, she'd done as her grandmother had always advised and been herself.

'You have acted your part of loving fiancée very well, *querida*. I for one was convinced.' This time, a steely undertone reverberated in every word, but still she walked, not daring to look up at him and certainly not daring to stop, to have those dark eyes fix on hers and see the truth of her feelings for him.

'It was what was expected, was it not, in order to convince the board that we were prepared to marry?' She quickened her step. Maybe if they left the park they could leave this topic behind.

'Then I applaud you. You even fooled me, especially when you were in my bed.'

She stopped and whirled round to face him. Didn't he have any idea that these last few days had not been about the deal? They had been about letting go, being herself—being with him, the man she'd fallen ever harder for. How dared he bring that up, make it sound as if she'd bartered with herself, sold her body, just to clear her father's debts?

'At least you cannot deny I have kept my part of the deal.' The angry words flew at him but to her utter annoyance her response amused him, serving only to make her even angrier.

Raul smiled as the glitter of anger sparkled in her eyes, far more dazzling than the ring she'd just given back to him. With the afternoon sun shining through the bare branches of the trees above them and then dancing in her hair, she looked so very beautiful. Once again, that need to have more, to find more with this woman, surged forwards. He savagely pushed it down, hid it behind a sharp retort.

'No, I cannot,' he said curtly. 'Even when we were alone you maintained the act of attraction, carried it through to a most satisfying conclusion.'

She paled and a spike of guilt lanced at him. This was the one and only woman he'd wanted to get close to, get to know better, and yet he was emotionally pushing her away, wounding her with his words. It just proved he wasn't a man who should settle down, who should be given the responsibility of someone's heart, someone's deepest emotions. Whether he liked it or not, he was far too much like his father.

'I despise you, Raul—for everything you have done.' She pulled herself free of his hold and began to march away.

'Where are you going, Lydia?'

He watched the sway of her hips in the white jeans that hugged her legs allowing him to see and appreciate her. It also reminded him how it felt to have them wrapped around his body as he'd made her his—even if it was only for the weekend.

She turned and faced him once more, her pretty face set in the firm grip of anger. 'Nothing would induce me to stay a moment longer in your company, Raul. I'm going back to London—today.'

For the briefest of seconds, he floundered, then control and coldness returned. 'You agreed we would return together.'

'I have things to attend to, Raul.' The ice in her voice chilled him far more than the winter wind that had begun to sweep through the park.

'What things?'

'I have dress selections to make.'

'Ah, but of course, the busy life of a socialite— shopping is your prime concern.' He couldn't keep the sarcasm from his voice as he walked towards her, closing the distance once again. Her green eyes glittered watchfully as he moved closer still. If he reached out now he could stroke the soft skin of her face, slide his finger beneath her chin, lifting it up, and then he would be able to kiss her.

'That just proves you don't know me at all.' Her angry words halted the desire-driven thoughts of kissing her once more.

'So, what is it you have hidden from me?' Suspicion slipped over him and he narrowed his eyes as she continued to glare challengingly up at him. 'Are you still the spoilt girl I first met, concerned only with parties and shopping?'

'I was almost seventeen, Raul. It's what teenagers do. Yes, I party sometimes, I'm also often out in London, but it is business, Raul. You of all people should know that necessity.' A hint of satisfaction spread over her face, forcing her lips to stretch into a smile.

'And what business would this be?' Now he was intrigued. He'd always thought there was more to Lydia Carter-Wilson than she allowed people to see, but why had she hidden it from him?

'I have several successful ladies' fashion boutiques, one in London and one in Paris. I had thought to open one here in Madrid. I even made a useful contact whilst shopping for the silver dress I wore to the party.'

He couldn't say anything; his mind had instantly gone back to Friday evening, to dancing so very close with her and then taking her home, where he'd removed the dress.

Lydia continued her self-satisfied attack as he struggled momentarily against the memory of that night. 'But that would mean running the risk of seeing you again, so I will forget that idea.'

'And why did you keep this from me as well as your ability to speak my language?' Finally, he pushed the erotic memory to one side.

'The truth?'

'Yes.'

'You hated me when we first met and it made me think my grandmother's advice was right—to just be myself.'

His mind raced back to that moment at the dinner party when they'd first met. The way she'd made him feel, the effect her smile had had on him had shocked him and he'd covered it all up with a brusque uninterested manner.

'So you learnt Spanish and formed a business because of that night?' Guilt rushed at him.

'I have worked hard to prove myself, to be my own person, and I was not about to allow my father, or you, to take that from me. As far as I was concerned his debts would be paid by the properties he'd hidden in my name and not my business. Of course now I know it would never have been enough.'

'And what if marriage had become necessary? What if you hadn't located my brother?'

'Then I would have married you, if it meant saving the one thing I'd worked hard for. My life. My independence.'

'So was this weekend a practice for the honeymoon?'

Fury leapt to her eyes; the smile that had lingered seductively on her lips disappeared. 'This weekend was a mistake. A very big mistake. Now, if you will excuse me, I need to pack and book a flight to London.'

'I have planned that we will go on my jet tomorrow.'

'You are, but I'm going now—alone.'

CHAPTER TEN

THE GREY RAIN-FILLED sky of London matched Raul's mood as he glared out of his hotel window at the skyline, impressive even in this weather. All last night he'd tossed and turned, haunted by the memory of one weekend with a woman who had changed his life far more than he cared to admit. Just as he refused to acknowledge that he missed her, that he hadn't wanted to let her go.

Yesterday, he'd watched Lydia march off through the park not realising how serious she was about leaving Madrid until they'd returned in silence to his apartment where she'd promptly booked a flight. The temptation to stop her, to try and make her stay, had been almost too much for him—until he'd reminded himself that such ideas were a sign of total weakness. Not only did he not indulge in such emotions, but she was the woman who had kept secrets from him, secrets that had not been hers to keep.

She'd packed, left and within an hour he had been alone. Silence had hung heavy around him as he'd brooded over their weekend, his rational thoughts accepting it had been exactly as she'd claimed. A mistake. For both of them. He'd allowed her to get close, expose depths of his emotions he'd never intended to be shown, only to find she was as manipulative and cold as him. Hell, what else had she lied about? Had all that talk of her family, her childhood been to lull him into a false sense of security whilst she dug deeper into his past?

With an angry growl he turned away from the view of London, feeling more like a caged animal. Coffee and distraction were what he needed right now. He had to focus his mind, put Lydia totally out of it. He had to forget her. Especially today. He was to meet his brother, the son his father had truly wanted. With a feral oath slipping from him, he left the luxurious hotel suite, intent on seeking the company of unknown businessmen at breakfast and the normality that had left his life the moment Lydia had entered it.

The aroma of strong coffee focused his mind as he sat at breakfast, although food was the last thing he wanted. The bitterness of the black liquid spiked his senses, bringing the controlled man he'd become back into play. Exactly what he needed to be, today of all days. He couldn't allow himself to dwell on the events of the weekend, not now at least.

In a bid for distraction he picked up one of the newspapers, but it wasn't the headline that caught his attention, it was the photo of Lydia looking every bit the socialite on a night out. Suspicion and a spark of lust slammed into him hard as he gritted his teeth firmly and looked at the image. A growl of Spanish slipped from him as he read the headline.

Blackmailed into an engagement by Spanish billionaire looking for unknown half-brother!

The paper shook as he held it, his fingers tightening on the offending pages until they hurt. She'd sold him out. Lydia had gone from his bed straight to the press. Was that why she'd been so keen to leave Madrid, to leave him? Before the headlines broke?

He shouldn't read it, shouldn't give it even the smallest bit of his attention, but his eyes began quickly to scan the words even though his emotions, and maybe even his heart, warned against it.

London heiress Lydia Carter-Wilson has been unable to keep the dark family secrets of Spanish business mogul Raul Peréz Valdez.

'Raul was shocked to discover he had an older brother,' a reliable source informed.

The only heir to his father's estate has just discovered the existence of a brother, who will now share the inheritance of his father's company, Banco de Torrez. The blackmailed bride-to-be is honouring a contract her father

*had signed with the late Maximiliano Valdez
in order to pay off family debts.*

*Legitimate son, Raul, seems more than
happy to marry instead of sharing his inheritance with his half-brother.*

A curse left his lips without any thought for those
around him. She'd even shamed her father. What
kind of a woman did that? A mercenary one who
only thought of herself.

Right at this moment he was trapped in a bubble
of anger. He'd trusted Lydia, allowed her into his
family and, if he was brutally honest, his emotions.
She'd got to him on a level he'd never known—and
then she'd done this.

He pulled out his phone and with savage satisfaction pressed Lydia's number. Infuriatingly, she didn't
answer and as the message system kicked in he almost cut the connection, but sense prevailed. The
sooner she realised he knew what she'd been up to,
the better, but first there was time for a little of her
own medicine. Deceit.

'Lydia. There are papers to sign for your father's
debt. I will see you at twelve forty-five, before I meet
Max at one.'

With a satisfied smile he ended the call. He had
no doubt she would be there. Just as he had no doubt
she would try and deny all knowledge of the article.
After all, hadn't she kept Max's whereabouts from

him for several days before enlightening him—only then she'd made seduction the main game plan? What would her plan be today?

It seemed Miss Carter-Wilson was as cold and calculating as he was and would do anything to extract herself from the debt her father had tied her to—but this time she'd gone too far. This time she'd played with the wrong man and for that she would pay.

Lydia's heart sank as she entered the smart hotel, the large Christmas tree mocking her as it sparkled. With Christmas a week away, carols filled the hotel with joy and happiness. She was far from feeling anything like that, knowing this meeting with Raul would be so much more difficult than that first one almost three weeks ago. She hung up her coat in the cloakroom and walked over to the mirror, where, feeling the need for more armour, she reapplied her lipstick then looked at her reflection.

She'd changed in the last three weeks. She might not look any different from the woman who had first met Raul, but she was. She'd had her heart broken—exactly what she'd spent all her adult life trying to avoid. Now, thanks to her father's bad business dealings and one impulsive weekend with Raul Valdez, she felt totally out of control even though she looked far from it. She took in a deep breath and smoothed her hands down the bold red skirt of the suit she'd spent time selecting this morning. Just as she had done on their first meeting, she'd dressed with care, wanting to exude a confidence she was far from feeling, and now she'd seen the headlines in today's papers she needed every bit of help she could get.

Had Raul seen them too?

He couldn't have seen it. He'd never have calmly left a message to meet her just to sign papers if he had. Would he?

He is capable of anything.

That thought echoed round in her mind as her heels tapped out a solitary beat across the elegant lobby towards the restaurant where Raul would soon meet his brother. The fact that he'd arranged to meet her so close to that meeting must surely mean all he wanted was a few papers signed. She clung to that hope as she entered the restaurant, strangely empty of any other dinners. When she saw him sitting calmly waiting for her at a table in the middle of the room, she knew that was a mistaken idea. He was dressed immaculately in a charcoal-grey suit, but nothing could detract from the air of superiority and total control he exuded.

He rose from his seat and stood waiting for her; the angry set of his handsome face left her in no doubt he had seen the headlines. Her futile hope slithered away, taking with it the remainder of her confidence as his dark eyes glared accusingly at her, his anger palpable even at this distance.

She walked towards him, her head held high, trying to match his strength, to show he didn't intimidate her at all. As she got closer her confidence faltered and she stopped halfway across the room, glad now that they were the only people there. She glanced around, just to check.

'I booked the entire restaurant to ensure I had the privacy I needed.' Raul sounded calm, approachable, but she wasn't fooled. She could detect the steely edge lurking beneath the surface. Calm he might be, but he was definitely far from approachable.

She turned to face him, looking into those dark eyes she'd lost her heart to, trying to bring confidence from deep within her. 'I got your message.'

'And I have seen your salacious kiss and tell in the papers this morning.' He went straight in for the kill, his voice now harder than the gleam of anger in his eyes, but she remained resolutely still, meeting his gaze and the accusation within it head-on. Inside she trembled but outside she was strong and defiant. The armour that had served her well for many years deflected most of the pain.

'I'm very sorry to disappoint, but I am not the source of your embarrassment.' She raised her brows at him in a show of high-handedness as she said that final word, then continued before he had a chance to say anything, 'Surely a man like you is used to sidestepping such stories in the papers.'

'About my lovers, yes.' He let the barbed words hang in the air and she refused to react, refused to think that one day she too could be linked to him as one of his lovers—exactly what she'd never wanted to be. 'About my fiancée, no.'

Fury boiled up inside her. 'I am not your fiancée. Not any longer. I kept my side of the deal.'

'On that I beg to differ.' The superiority in his voice rankled but she maintained a stony silence, forcing him to continue. 'You have shared the story of my half-brother with someone and now it is everywhere. You broke the terms of our contract, Lydia.'

'I have not shared it with anyone,' she blurted out, hurt that he could accuse her of such a thing after all they'd shared.

Raul laughed. A cold, cynical laugh, which sent a shiver of worry all over her, chilling her to the core. 'Do you really expect me to believe that, *querida*? You were so strong-willed, so against any kind of affair, yet suddenly you changed. You became a passionate woman intent only on desire. You used the mutual attraction between us to drag out more of the story.'

'I did not.' Indignation fired the retort at him but as he moved away from the table and came towards her, his dark eyes watching her closely, she regretted the outburst. Was that what he thought their weekend affair had been? When she'd been enjoying the gentle truce between them, the deeper understanding she'd gained of him as they'd talked about their pasts, he'd been satisfying a more basic need. How stupid had she been to fall for his act of vulnerability, to feel sorry for him?

He came very close to her, walking around her, his shoulder almost touching hers, as if they were about to start dancing. Not a slow sedate dance like the night of the party, but a wild passionate dance. A tango filled with anger.

Quickly she looked away and wished that other diners were here. At least it would stop the intimacy of this meeting, but that was not possible because Raul had, yet again, manipulated the situation to suit him. What kind of man booked out an entire restaurant?

One in total control—of everything.

'You begged me to take you to my bed.' The hardness in his eyes didn't match the silky seductive sound of his voice and a tremor of awareness sizzled over her, Why did she still feel like this? How could he still have such a hold on her—on her heart?

'I felt sorry for you.' She was shocked at that last thought, her gaze met the fury of his and, once again, she wished the impetuous words unsaid. Still she held his gaze, her chin lifted mutinously in a desperate attempt to hide the real reason she'd wanted to be with him, hide the love that had been impossible to ignore as it had blossomed during those two blissful days.

'So, it was pity sex.' He turned and walked away from her and she could see the tension in his shoulders as clearly as she could feel it bouncing around the empty restaurant. Then he whirled round to face her. 'That is even worse.'

'I don't care what kind of sex it was, Raul; I did not sell your story. Just tell me what was so important so I can go before your brother arrives. I will leave and we will never have to see one another again. You can move on with your life, safe in the knowledge you have safeguarded the company, destroyed my father and kept all you wanted.'

Around the room the air prickled with challenge as she glared at him. She wanted to tell him it was far from pity sex, that it had been much more about falling for him—falling in love. But that would be futile. This man didn't want love in his life. Inwardly, she groaned. How had she been so stupid? To think this man could ever feel anything for her?

'I'm afraid that will not be possible, Lydia.' The tone of his voice had changed again. He sounded dangerous and icily calm as he moved back towards her.

'What do you mean?' She held her ground, stood firm in the high black patent heels she'd chosen for added height, added confidence.

'What I mean, Lydia, is that you have broken the agreement you signed. The one that stated you would not share any information with anyone else.' Menace laced every word as he stopped a short distance from her, as if he didn't dare come any closer. He hated her now. She could see it in his eyes, hear it in his words and feel it surrounding her.

'Why would I do that?' From the moment she'd arrived in Madrid she'd become caught up in Raul's story and even more caught up in the man himself. She'd wanted to help, wanted to be the one who made a difference to his life.

'You tell me. I have lost a lucrative contract over this and who knows? I may well have lost my brother before I gained him.' Pain lashed through her. He didn't care at all that they'd lost the closeness they'd found in Madrid or that they were losing each other with each angry word he spoke.

'I'm sorry, but it wasn't me.' Outwardly, she remained strong. Detached. Inside, she was falling to pieces and she wanted this moment to end.

'I don't need your damn pity—in any form.' He rounded on her and she closed her eyes against the agony that was ripping her heart into shreds. How had she ever thought it might be possible that one day they could become more than just an affair? She couldn't stay a moment longer and listen to him, feel how much he hated her.

'And I don't need this.' With a toss of her head, her hair flinging out around her, she turned and started to walk away.

'If my brother doesn't arrive at one as arranged, then all you have done will have been in vain. Your moment of glory—or is it revenge?—will be for nothing.' Raul's steady voice halted her steps and she turned to face him. Was he holding her responsible for Max not turning up?

She looked at her watch. Less than ten minutes until Max should arrive. But what if he didn't?

'If my brother doesn't arrive, your father's debts will remain unpaid and our engagement deal will stand.' His words were hard and grating, his handsome face full of anger.

'You can't force me to marry you.' She matched his anger as she flung the words at him.

'I can and I will.'

Lydia looked to the door of the restaurant, hoping to see a man striding through, but nothing. 'No, I've done all I can do. I've found him for you. It's not my fault if he doesn't show up.'

'Isn't it?' The accusation was clear. He blamed her. She looked again at her watch. In five minutes she would know her fate. In five minutes she would have lost the man she'd fallen in love with, because whatever happened next she knew, without doubt, that he hated her.

Raul watched Lydia as she looked at the time. He saw the colour drain from her face and a brief wave of compassion surged over him. Savagely, he pushed it back. He didn't have room for compassion or any other kind of emotion that would make him want to go and take Lydia in his arms.

Any moment now his brother would walk into the restaurant and he would have to face the man who had taken his place in his father's affections even before he himself had been born.

'I should go.' Lydia's words rushed him back to the present.

'You will stay, Lydia. If he doesn't turn up then—' Raul's words were cut off by the noise of the door opening and his heart thumped as he looked beyond Lydia to see a member of hotel staff entering the room.

'Your guest is here, sir.'

All he could hear was the beat of his pulse in his ears and then his amazingly calm voice. 'Show him in.'

'It is just as well you booked the entire restaurant.' Lydia's remark gave him an anchorage as he waited for his brother to arrive.

'*Sí*, I prefer to conduct my affairs in private— unlike you.' The barb of his reply made those beautiful green eyes widen, just as they'd done that night they'd become lovers when he'd finally slipped the silver dress from her gorgeous body.

Why was he thinking about that now? He'd known she would be a distraction, which was why he'd let her walk away from him, let her think she had the upper hand. But that damned story she'd sold had changed that. Now she would pay for her loose tongue.

'I didn't sell that story, Raul.' Her gaze locked with his and despite the defiance in her stance, in the proud tilt of her chin, he could hear the pleading in her voice, a plea that distracted him from all other thought.

'Then who the hell did?' A deep male voice crashed

into the tension that had built between him and
Lydia, as if striking all ten pins on a bowling alley
in one fatal blow.

He heard Lydia gasp and drag in a deep breath
as he turned and looked his brother in the eye for
the first time. It was like looking at himself and he
clenched his teeth hard; the hope that his father had
got it all wrong vanished with one glittering look
from his firstborn son.

'It certainly wasn't me.' Lydia began to speak
again, fast bubbling words, which as far as he was
concerned underlined her guilt in red, not because
she had genuinely wanted to help him because of her
deepening feelings for him. 'I want the debt settled.
I want out of your life.'

'Then get out, Lydia,' Raul snapped without even
looking at her. Now was not the time for Lydia's nervous chatter.

His brother's gaze didn't leave his face, didn't break
the contact and there was no way he was going to
back down, give this man the upper hand. It seemed
an eternity as he stood there assessing and being assessed by the half-brother who had taken his place
in his father's affections, who'd become the only son
he'd ever wanted.

He should hate him for it.

Lydia moved closer to him. Every nerve in his
body felt it—heightened to even the smallest movement from this woman. It wasn't right that she had
such power over him. He heard the crinkle of paper

but remained resolutely locked in eye combat with his half-brother. He couldn't bring himself to think his name, much less say it. Not whilst the anger and pain of his childhood years surged through him.

'You should have this.' Lydia's whispered words finally caught his attention and he looked at her, then at the old, discoloured envelope she held out to him. 'It's from your mother.'

In that moment it was just the two of them—him and the woman who had slipped under his defensive barrier and into his heart, rendering him as weak as a newborn colt. The very same woman who'd betrayed him in the most spectacular way. And it hurt—like hell. He'd watched his mother's heartache at his father's betrayal as he'd grown from a boy into a man, seen it all around him and vowed never, ever, to be the victim of such emotions.

Now he too knew the bitter taste of betrayal from a loved one.

He took the envelope in a firm, decisive move then looked into those green eyes he'd thought so sexy, so full of something special for him. His lip curled into a snarl. 'I never want to see you again. Ever.'

Lydia burst through the door of the restaurant, desperate to leave the charged atmosphere of the room. She couldn't bear to stand there and see the anger in Raul's eyes, anger that made him despise her.

She swiped at a tear as it sprang from her eye and pulled all her anger to the fore, smothering the need to cry. 'Damn Christmas tree.' She brushed her hair back with both hands and raised her chin as she glared at the offending fir tree, decked out in gold with twinkling lights. 'What are you looking so happy about?'

'Are you okay?' A female voice came from behind her and Lydia whirled round to see a woman sitting in one of the large comfortable armchairs of the foyer, looking anything but comfortable if her perched position on the edge of the seat was anything to go by.

'Y-yes. Sorry,' Lydia stammered, realising how silly she must have looked to the glamorous redhead as she'd rushed out and begun her tirade at the Christmas tree. 'It's that time of year for stress overload, I guess.'

'Tell me about it,' the other woman said and Lydia relaxed a little, feeling as if she'd met a kindred spirit. 'A man?'

'The very same.' Lydia smiled, noticing how pale the redhead looked beneath her heavily applied make-up, as if she too was trying to hide something.

The woman smiled, but as raised male voices echoed from the restaurant both women looked at the door. For a moment Lydia wondered if she should say something. Was the beautiful woman waiting for Raul's brother? She decided against it. Raul was nothing to do with her any more. She'd found his brother and had unlocked the funds that would pay off her father's debt. She was free to go.

With that thought racing in her mind she rushed from the hotel, conscious of her hurried footsteps echoing after her and even feeling the redhead's curious gaze. Or was she just being fanciful? Was she in such a heightened state of emotions she wasn't thinking clearly?

The cold December wind took her breath away as she stood on the streets, the London traffic whizzing by, oblivious to the turmoil she was in. People passed her, some bumping her as she walked slowly in a daze of disbelief, not even aware of where she was going. Everyone around her seemed to be caught up in the buzz of Christmas and all she could do was think about what she'd lost.

The man she loved hated her. She'd seen it in his eyes. There was no doubt.

Christmas Eve was a week away. Now was no time to be nursing a broken heart. She pulled her coat tighter around her in an attempt to keep the cold at bay, but inside she was already frozen, her heart turned to ice by one look of contempt from Raul, and his last words played in her head like a Christmas carol turned sour.

'I never want to see you again. Ever.'

CHAPTER ELEVEN

RAUL COULDN'T COMPREHEND how alike he and Max were. There was no disputing they were brothers. It wasn't just the dark hair, which Max wore shorter, or the piercingly dark eyes, but the way he stood. Every line in his body was poised and commanding. Raul had not only met his brother, but his match, of that he was in no doubt, but right now he was far too angry with Lydia for her deception.

Because of her he'd lost a big deal and she'd caused him and Max unnecessary embarrassment. He wanted to believe she hadn't sold his story, that she hadn't used their passionate affair in order to gain all the information she could about the story of his brother and his father's double life, but it was just too coincidental. She'd gone from not wanting anything to do with him to seeking a passionate affair. He'd thought it had been desire driven, but he'd been wrong. Very wrong.

'Was that necessary?' his brother's voice fired accusingly at him. 'There was no need to be so hard on her.'

'Don't you dare presume that as my older brother you can tell me what I can and can't do.' Raul hurled the angry words back at Max. Thanks to Lydia and her indiscretion, this whole meeting had catapulted out of control. He couldn't even think clearly at the moment, saying the first thing that came to him in such an uncontrolled way, he didn't even recognise himself.

'Now we get to the crux of it.' Max strode towards him, the same purposeful strides he would use if he weren't rooted to the spot with shock and anger at the sudden realisation that Lydia had gone. Not just left the hotel, but gone. Out of his life for good.

Focus, he demanded himself. Now was not the time to reminisce over a love affair that had ended. Now was the time to focus on his future, to move forward from the lies his father had inflicted on him—and Max. To do the one thing his father had thought him incapable of—welcoming his brother into his life.

'That minor detail has nothing to do with it,' he shot back at Max, instantly regretting the anger in his words.

'Then you had better tell me what the hell it is you want from me so that you can go and sort out your love life.' Max's dark eyes, so like his own, pinned him to the spot and he resented his brother's inference that he and Lydia were lovers.

'We are not lovers.' He glared angrily at his brother, refusing to accept that maybe he was right. Damn him, he'd been in his life all of five minutes and already he was telling him what to do.

'That's not how it looked to me.' Max flicked an eyebrow up and a trickle of calm began to defuse the angry tension that arced between them like an ugly steel bridge, connecting them, connecting their past and their future, yet neither daring to cross it.

Raul sighed. 'I didn't ask you to come here to talk about me and Lydia—'

'I should hate you right now,' Max said, cutting off his words, blatantly attempting to take back control. He also echoed his own feelings exactly. He too should hate Max. Hate him for being the son his father always wanted, hate him for being given his father's name and most of all hate him for denying him his father's love.

But Max hadn't had a father's love either. He hadn't seen his father since he was eight years old, if all Carlos had told him was true.

Raul frowned. How did Carlos know so much? 'And do you? Hate me?'

'No.' Max turned and walked away. 'Neither of us are to blame. There is only one man who can take the blame for this, and, as always, he's too much of a coward to deal with it himself. He's left us to deal with the aftermath. Just as he walked away from my mother and I.'

Raul knew he was scowling as he digested this

nugget about his brother's childhood. The tone of his voice, the way he referred to their father gave away so much. Was it possible he too had suffered the effects of being the son of a man incapable of love for his son?

'Did he ever contact you again?' Raul had to know, had to hear it for himself.

'No—and for that I am grateful. My life was better without him.' Max's voice was hard. Controlled. But he spoke the truth, Raul didn't need any convincing of that.

'So, brother, where do we go from here?' Raul asked, knowing that whatever he did now he had to get Max on side, had to get him to accept his share of the inheritance his father had left equally between them—especially as he'd turned Lydia out of his life so harshly and she was the only other hope of paying the debt the board wanted settled.

'I'm not big on emotional commitment.' Max moved closer to him, echoing his own sentiments exactly. 'The love of a father, or even a woman, is overrated as far as I am concerned.'

Raul smiled, accepting they were already so alike. 'My sentiments precisely.'

'The young lady seemed pretty certain she didn't sell the story, but someone did.' Was Max accusing him?

'I lost a big deal because of it. I'd hardly do that.'

Max's brows rose, in a way that was like looking

at himself in the mirror. 'Then I suggest we work together to find out just who has it in for us.

'The media will be watching closely to see what happens next. There are probably bets on somewhere as to what we will do, but I'll wager that nobody, least of all our so-called father, would expect us to leave the past exactly where it is and move forwards—together.'

Raul held out his hand to shake on the deal Max was offering. It was far more than he'd hoped for, but if Max could put aside the past, so could he. 'Brothers.'

'Brothers,' Max replied and took his hand, their gazes locking. Then to Raul's relief and shock, Max let go of his hand and slapped him on the back. 'Brothers.'

Lydia had known exactly what she needed to do as she left Raul and his brother glaring like angry bulls at one another. She'd hailed a black cab to the station for the next train to Oxford. This time her father would face up to what he'd done. This time she was well and truly in charge. This time he'd pay. Not just for her, but for Raul—and Max.

Meeting Raul for the first time had made her grow up. Spending the weekend as his lover had given her clarity. Thinking of him spiked her heart with pain. How had she fallen in love with a man who could use her as savagely as her father had done?

She pushed the thought aside as the train pulled out of the station and a bitter December wind whistled down the platform as she wondered if she'd done the right thing.

Of course you have. He can't get away with not paying his debt.

The short taxi ride from the station to her father's home, one she'd hardly spent any time at recently, gave her just enough time to pull the last bit of confidence she had left and ready herself for seeing her father. Once that was done, she could go home and sleep away the pain of her broken heart, knowing she'd done all she could to make things right. Although they'd never be right for her again.

'I wasn't expecting you so close to Christmas.' Her father's voice boomed at her as he raised his head from whatever it was he was engrossed in at his desk. She heard the door being clicked shut as his maid retreated. Had she sensed the power of his daughter's determination?

'And I wasn't expecting to be made a scapegoat for your so-called deals.' She bit back a tirade she'd love to shower on him, wanting the implications of what she'd just said to sink in first. Would he defend himself or her?

'Ah.'

'Yes, ah.' She walked towards the desk, looking him in the eye and not missing the startled widening of his. He might not have been expecting to see her today, but he'd certainly never thought she'd be so mutinous.

'I thought you'd come to tell me you are about to marry the Valdez heir or, judging by the headlines today, I'd hazard a guess it's to congratulate me on a cunning plan which has made you a very wealthy woman and saved my neck.'

'How could you?' Her anger erupted, mixed together with the pent-up grief of losing the man she loved, even though deep down she knew she'd never had him at all. To him their time together had been merely a diversion. All that hurt tipped out onto her father. 'You used me. How could you? I will never forgive you.'

'Now hang on a minute.' He jumped up from his chair, papers sliding to the floor, his face red with anger. 'You now have properties worth millions.'

He'd walked right into her trap. 'Do I?'

'I did it for you, Lyd.' She hated it when he shortened her name and bit back the retort she'd like to hurl at him. He had to think she was softening, that she was complying with what he'd obviously planned from the outset.

'So I can do what I want with them?' she asked thoughtfully as he sat back down, looking relaxed again, believing he'd smoothed the rough water. 'Are you sure?'

'Quite sure, Lyd.' She smarted again beneath the fake endearment. 'Spend Christmas and New Year in the sun, then once the dust has settled you can transfer them back to me and we will have made millions. It can be our little investment.'

How devious could he get? How had she never noticed before just what he was like?

Because you have grown up.

'I might just do that,' she said with a smile on her face that was so hard to achieve. 'In actual fact I think I will fly out to one of them tomorrow.'

'That's my girl. I knew you'd see sense.' The condescending tone sickened her but she played her part to the end.

'Now, if you will excuse me, I've got packing to do.'

As her father's laughter trailed after her Lydia felt numb. She had lost her father long ago, and today she'd lost the man she'd fallen in love with. But the truth was she'd never been loved by Raul.

'Have a good time and Merry Christmas.' The belated words trailed down the wood-panelled hallway of his latest home and briefly she longed to slip back in time, to the home she'd grown up in, before her parents had parted company and she'd gone to live with her grandmother. But just as going back to the time she'd spent with Raul was impossible, so was going back to the small window of happiness in her childhood. The only way was forwards, even if it was fraught with pain.

'I will.' If he only knew what she really had planned for his little *investment*, he wouldn't be so happy. First she would call her solicitor and get enough of the properties transferred into Raul's name to cover the debt that, as far as she was concerned, her father still owed. After that she would sell the rest and give it all to charity. She wanted nothing to do with them. Only then did she feel she could move on from her disastrous first taste of love.

Raul had gone straight to the bar after his brother had left and ordered a whisky. He'd needed the hot fire of the amber liquid, not because of the way things had gone with Max, but because of the way things had gone with Lydia.

As the image of her lovely face swam into his mind he remembered the envelope she'd all but thrust at him and pulled it from his pocket. He placed it on the bar and ordered a second drink. The young woman behind the bar smiled at him as she placed the drink next to the envelope, but it was a smile wasted on him now. There was only one woman's smile he wanted to see but he had to remember what she'd done, the story she'd sold.

Unable to believe the duplicity of Carlos, the only other person who knew the secrets of the past, or his blatant admission when challenged, he and Max had come up with their own exclusive to sell to the press. The proceeds were to be split equally between their favoured charity projects of Sports for Youngsters and Community Rebuild. The fact that they both headed charities proved yet another similarity between them and highlighted just how different they both were from their father. Except that Raul shared the fatal flaw of being unable to love, to give his heart to anyone.

He reached for his second drink, then paused, his hand over the envelope. Was he ready to read its contents? What was in it that was so bad his mother had never told him? He cursed beneath his breath. Why hadn't he ever broached the subject with her? He ignored the drink and the oblivion it lured him with and picked up the envelope.

Around him the bar became busy with Christmas shoppers and businessmen and women. The noise level rose as everyone chatted against the backdrop of traditional carols, but he didn't hear any of it. The forthcoming festive season was the last thing on his mind as he read, first the torn pages of what must have been his mother's journal and then a letter, written to him by his mother, dated on his tenth birthday.

Both told the story of his father's deception, of the brother he would never know and of her family's insistence that they remain married or she would be disinherited and his double life exposed. Now her acceptance of his father's behaviour made sense and the realisation that her story was out there in the world of the media made talking to her essential.

He'd rather do it face to face, be able to see her expression and be there to offer comfort, but London was nearly a three-hour flight from Madrid. There was only one option, so he moved away from the bar, to a quieter corner and took out his phone, waiting whilst the call he least wanted to make connected.

Just as he wondered if he'd done the right thing his mother's voice sounded across the miles, her Spanish words grounding him. 'I was expecting your call.'

'Then you will know why I am calling.' He didn't ask, but made it clear he was stating a fact. He had no wish to hurt his mother, to drag up what must be a painful past, but he had to know the truth and it seemed, if nothing else, Lydia had been right about one thing. His mother was the best person to ask.

'As soon as I saw you and Lydia together I knew it was time.' Raul frowned. Where was this leading? Whatever it was she had to tell him had nothing to do with Lydia now and he was about to say just that when his mother spoke over his thoughts. 'I could see how much she loves you—and how much you love her.'

He should correct her, should tell her she'd got it all wrong. How could anyone have imagined there was love between them? 'I need to know why you kept the truth of Max from me.'

'When you were young it was to try and mend things between you and your father, to try and keep the family together—for you, not anyone or anything else.'

A noisy group of couples sat at the table next to him, full of the joys of the festive season, but he couldn't end the call now, he had to continue. 'There was never any love lost between me and my father and now I know why. He already had a son—and had given him his name.'

'I knew about the baby, but not the name,' she carried on, her voice beginning to waver, and he wished there weren't so many miles between them for this conversation. 'I only found that out when his double life was exposed and you were so young and not getting on with your father, I couldn't give you more reasons to fall out with him.'

'You must have known it would come out?' Raul snapped, ignoring the curious glance from the party next to him, turning his back on them and their happiness. He picked up his glass of whisky, about to take a long swig, when his mother answered.

'That's why I waited until you had the support of a woman who loves you.'

He cursed loudly in Spanish. 'Lydia and I are not in love. We were forced into marriage because of a clause in the damn will. Her father's debts and my father's need to drag up the past forced us into an engagement.'

He heard his mother gasp. 'He did that to you?'

'Unless I found Max and shared the inheritance. Yes, he did that.' Raul's voice was granite hard and he tightened his grip around the glass so much he thought he might actually break it. 'With help from Carlos.'

'Carlos? I can't believe he would stoop so low, but your father, yes.'

'There will be no wedding, Mother. Lydia found Max, thanks to the information you gave her, and unlocked the funds Father had set aside as a reward for acknowledging Max as my older brother. He gambled on the fact that her father wouldn't repay the debt and that I'd rather track down his firstborn son than get married.'

It angered Raul to think that his father had known him so well, played him to the very end, but in taking up that challenge he'd hurt others. His mother for one, but the fact that he'd hurt Lydia enough to make her hate him was too much.

'He'd engineered it all, knowing he wouldn't have long left?' The shock in his mother's voice was so clear he could imagine her sitting in her favourite chair and the expression on her face.

'Every last detail.'

'None of that changes the fact that Lydia loves you. Don't lose her, Raul, don't throw away your happiness.' His mother pleaded with him and now he was glad he wasn't standing before her. How long would she keep up this particular argument?

'I am not in love with Lydia.' He snapped the words in rapid Spanish, again causing others to look his way.

'Then maybe you are more like your father than you imagine.'

Raul gritted his teeth. He wasn't having this conversation. Not now. Not here like this. Not when he'd just sent Lydia out of his life for good. 'I can't talk any more.'

'Talk to her, Raul—for me.'

He cut the call without giving his mother any further opportunity to increase the pain that raged inside him like a wild animal, pain from the deceit of the past as well as the deceit of the present.

He downed the whisky in one go and then slammed the glass down on the table. Lydia loved him? Not possible. She was as cold and calculating as he was—and also now financially very well off with her new property portfolio. Did that mean they were well matched? Or was she hiding the real Lydia as much as he kept his true emotions hidden?

He thought back to their time together in Madrid and ultimately to that passionate weekend. He had been happy then, even forgetting the need to find Max as he'd lived the lie of being Lydia's lover. But had it been a lie? Was the elusive emotion of love the reason he'd been so happy in Madrid, so like a completely different version of himself?

As Christmas carols began to fill the bar again, jingling with merriment, he finally had the nerve to question himself, question just what it was that had sparked into life between him and Lydia from their very first meeting here in London. He thought back to the hard and cruel words he'd hurled at her just moments before she'd run out of his life. He could still hear the feral growl in his voice, as if it were being played alongside the bright and cheery carols.

An angry curse slipped from him and he strode to the bar, ordering another whisky and swigging it back in one. He glared at his reflection in the mirrored wall of the bar, distorted by the array of optics. He'd been a fool to think Lydia would betray him. He knew she would never willingly drag herself through the mire of the press and was as much a victim as he and Max. He also knew now that the passion they had shared, one so strong and powerful, like nothing he'd ever known, was not born out of lust—but love.

The unthinkable had happened. He'd fallen in love.

Lydia Carter-Wilson, his fake fiancée, was the woman he wanted to marry, the woman he wanted to have children with—and he'd sent her away.

Raul left the bar, the cold wind whipping at his coat as he crossed the busy street, dashing in front of black cabs. It wasn't the whisky that had dulled his senses, making him careless, but the loss of the woman he loved.

CHAPTER TWELVE

FIVE DAYS HAD passed since Lydia had last seen Raul and still his words echoed in her mind, haunting her day and night. The expression on his face, the pure anger directed at her, was there each time she closed her eyes. Whatever she did she couldn't get away from him, from thinking about him or from the misguided love she still had for him. But she had to and in an attempt to move on, to rebuild her life, she'd chosen to be at work, needing the distraction of ladies wanting glamorous party dresses, and, with only one weekend until Christmas, it was sure to be busy.

She'd read the headlines this morning, seen the picture of happiness Raul and Max had portrayed to the world through the lens of the press. They were pleased to have found each other and would move forwards together in a business they had both inherited as well as continue with their own businesses. It all looked too good to be true and she wondered how much of it was indeed true. How much of it was yet more business deals struck, more acting the part for the media or board of directors?

Was Max as hard and mercenary as Raul? Judging by what she'd seen just a few days ago, the stand-off she'd left in full swing, she suspected they were very alike. They were both hard and emotionless men who would stop at nothing to get what they wanted.

The door of the salon opened, bringing with it the noise of traffic from Knightsbridge and a rush of crisp, cold air. She didn't turn immediately, but continued with her task of ensuring the party dresses were displayed to their full potential, giving the customer a moment or two to browse. A few moments later, she pinned on a smile she was far from feeling and turned to greet her customer.

That smile froze on her lips as she took in Raul, standing in all his male magnificence in the centre of her boutique, watching her with narrowed eyes. What did he want now? Hadn't he hurt her enough already?

'I have nothing to say to you, Raul.' She glared at him, daring him to stay, daring him to try and say anything to her. She'd cried so much already and had been totally weakened by his cold words as she'd tried to explain what had happened. She'd been on the brink of telling him that she'd never do such a thing to the man she loved, but, thankfully, his curt remark had cut that off midsentence, reminding her how foolhardy she'd been.

At least she hadn't been given the chance to tell him how she really felt, that she loved him and all she'd done had been out of love for him.

'But I have much to say to you, Lydia.' He didn't move; like a matador preparing for the fight, he stood firm, his strong maleness so out of place amidst the sparkle of the dresses.

'Nothing I want to hear.' She turned her back on him and picked up a gold sequined top, hoping he would turn and leave. She closed her eyes against the pain as she heard his steady footsteps. He was leaving. So much for wanting to speak to her.

She listened, shock coursing through her as the bolt slid on the door of the shop and then the blind rolled slowly and purposefully down. What was he doing? She whirled round, still clutching the gold top, her fingers crushing the sequins as she pressed them hard around the padded hanger.

The self-satisfied expression on his face intensified her anger and as his brows rose in that familiar and very alluring way, her heart thumped wildly. Why did he have to look so sexy, so completely gorgeous?

'The boutique is *not* closed.' She fired the words at him, infusing them with anger, desperate to sound firm and as in control as he appeared to be.

'It is very much closed. At least until I have said what I came to say.' He moved towards her and she watched, unable to take in what was happening or why he was here.

'My assistant will be back very soon.'

'She can wait.' The curt reply was as sharp as it was hard, but she glared at him, meeting the challenge that was very definitely in his eyes head-on.

'Very well. Say your piece and then leave. I have no wish to prolong this any longer than is needed.' She tried to make her voice portray how uninterested she was to hear what he had to say, but her last words wavered, giving away the turmoil of emotions she now had rushing through her. But then Raul was the steeliest and most unemotional man she had ever met and she doubted he'd pick up on her minefield of emotions.

His brows rose and the flicker of a smile pulled at his lips so briefly she thought she'd imagined it. He moved closer. 'I know that you didn't sell the story.'

Relief flooded her, but it was short-lived and she couldn't smile at him, didn't want to take his harshly delivered statement as an apology. 'So after everything you said to me in front of your brother, you think you can just turn up and say you'd made a mistake without a word of apology?'

'I have just said I was wrong.' His eyes hardened with the glitter of anger as he spoke. Well, he wasn't the only one who was angry.

'But you can't say you are sorry, can you, Raul?' She challenged him, pushed him to feel something. 'You can't say it because you don't feel it. You are so cold, so emotionless.'

'Being so emotionless, as you say, is what has made me so successful.' The retort sparked back at her and she glared at him. 'But if it makes you happy, then I am sorry. I now know you did not sell the story.'

She wanted more than that. Wanted to hear him say he couldn't live without her, that he should never have sent her away—that he loved her. She wanted him to feel something for her.

'And how did you come to this conclusion?' The terse words slipped easily from her lips. She was finally getting her emotions under control, managing to hide them away, and discussing the story was safer than anything else right now.

'The source was revealed to me.' He paused, as if waiting for her to say something, to respond, and she wasn't going to disappoint him. 'My father had enlisted the help of a close friend, a member of the board, but he proved to be as corrupt as my father and his silence has now been assured with a hefty payment.'

'Of course. Power and wealth can buy you just about anything, can't it?' Lydia's words, spoken in perfect Spanish, cracked harder than any whip as they lashed at him. But she was right—and she despised him for it. Pain slashed through him, cutting deeper than a sword. He'd never known anything like it. To hear such an accusation from the woman he loved—and in his own language.

'Not always.' He tried to gentle his emotions, to remember why he was here in the first place. Another war of words with Lydia wouldn't achieve anything other than to push her further out of his reach. The exact opposite of what he wanted.

'Ah, so there is something the mighty Raul Valdez wants that money can't buy.' The sarcasm of her words stung the wound his pain had opened and he gritted his teeth against it and the truth of her words.

'Yes.' The word sounded feral, even to him, and the lift of her delicate brows made it clear she thought so too. Hell. Why couldn't he just tell her? Why couldn't he say the words? Tell her that he wanted her—loved her? Had he been so void of emotion for so long that he could no longer say what he felt? This was harder than any deal he'd ever won or lost, but, whatever happened, he couldn't lose, not now. 'There is something I very much want.'

Her eyes narrowed and she put the gold top back on the rail, averting her gaze and deliberately taking her time. When she looked back at him her expression was as neutral as the day he'd first seen her in the restaurant in London. She gave nothing away as once again she spoke in Spanish, reminding him of that dinner party, punishing him for his hurtful remark. 'And what has this to do with me?'

He moved towards her and her eyes widened, blinking rapidly a few times, but she didn't step away, didn't break eye contact. 'It is you I want, Lydia.'

He'd said it. He'd actually admitted that he wanted someone, needed someone. For the first time in his life, after years of hiding his heart, hiding his emotions, he'd told the woman he loved, the woman he wanted, just how he felt.

'No.' Lydia glared at him, angry sparks in her eyes, deepening the green of them, making them so intense that he couldn't help but look into them. He saw pain behind the anger. Pain he'd caused. But there was something else.

'No?' Incredulity at the show of emotions in her eyes almost made saying anything impossible. 'What do you mean, "No"?'

'I mean I have no intention of having any more to do with you. I was a fool to think we ever had any kind of future and even more of a fool to think that…' The passion of her outburst, again in Spanish, surprised him, as did the sudden faltering of her words. It was the only hint that his mother had been right, that this woman did feel something for him and was as good at hiding that as he was.

'To think what, Lydia?' he jumped in quickly, not wanting that small opening to pass by. It might be the only chance to find out how this woman truly felt, to find out if she had the same feelings for him as he had for her.

'That you cared about me.' She marched past him,

her shoulder brushing against his upper arm she moved so quickly. He heard the blind being pulled roughly up, heard the bolt being slid back into place and as he turned to her he saw her wrench open the door. 'But I was wrong.'

'Is that why you lodged the deeds of most of the properties with your solicitor, putting them all into my name?' He watched her as she lifted her chin, mutinous defiance filling her body as she stood there by the open boutique door, angry green eyes blazing at him.

'I honour my debts.' Defiance sparked like flint on stone in every word she said, starting a fire of emotions. 'Fully.'

'And your promises?' He raised his voice as he fought against the noise of the London traffic. 'Do you honour those too?'

'Of course I do. Now please go. Leave.'

He took a few steps to her, getting so close he could smell her perfume, the same as she'd worn at the party. Memories of the dance leapt to life in his mind, hotly followed by those of that passionate night when she'd been his.

'Leave. Go,' she said in Spanish, the words hard and cruel, twisting the knife in his heart. The finality of the words too much, but he couldn't go.

He took her hand from the door, his eyes locked with hers. 'You made a promise to me, Lydia. You were my fiancée.'

'That wasn't a promise.' Her voice was barely a whisper as she looked up at him, her eyes searching his. Was she looking for the same emotion in his that he was searching for in hers? Love. 'That was nothing more than a deal—or blackmail.'

'And if it became something more?' Tentatively he asked, ignoring the laughter from a couple passing by the shop, his attention firmly fixed on the woman he loved.

'It could never be more, Raul. You can't give yourself or your heart. You made that very clear. We had an affair, nothing more, but it's over.'

She shut the boutique door, the traffic noise dimming as she glared accusingly at him. She was right. He couldn't give his heart, couldn't allow himself to feel any soft emotions and definitely not love. But that had been before she'd turned his world upside down, shaking his heart into life.

Lydia turned from him, taking his silence as agreement, but as she walked away he knew he couldn't leave it there, couldn't give up.

'I was wrong.' He strode after her, wanting to reach for her, wanting to force her to look at him, to listen to him.

She stood very still, her back to him, and the seconds ticked by as he waited. Finally, she turned and looked up at him, weariness in her eyes. 'So was I.'

He was losing. The one battle in his life he had to win and he knew he was losing it—losing her. He

had to say the words he'd never said to anyone. It was
the only hope he had of making her understand. 'I
was wrong, Lydia.'

He paused and looked into those lovely green
eyes, saw her blink quickly, as if tears threatened.
'I was wrong because I love you, Lydia.'

Lydia looked at the man she loved, a man she'd
thought incapable of saying those words to her. But
saying them wasn't meaning them. 'It's too late.'

She wanted to walk away, wanted to avoid the
power of those devilishly sexy eyes, but she couldn't.
All she could do was stand there and look up at him.

He shook his head. 'No, Lydia. It's not too late.
I've been a fool, yes, but it's not too late.'

'I'm sorry I messed everything up just before your
brother arrived, but most of all I'm sorry that my father ever got us into this mess.'

'I'm not. I've found my brother *and* the woman I
love. The woman I want to be my wife.'

He was offering her everything she wanted, everything she'd dreamed of, but this was Raul Valdez, billionaire businessman who got anything he
wanted by fair means or foul. She stepped back from
him, away from the temptation of his potent masculinity, away from the need to feel his lips on hers
just one more time. Not that once more would ever
be enough, not when she loved him so completely.

A shaky laugh slipped from her. 'That's not possible. We can't.'

'We can,' he said and moved towards her, so close now that she could smell the freshness of his morning shower. Gently he reached out and cupped her cheek in his hand and she fought the urge to lean into the caress, to believe what he was saying was real.

'I've paid my debts, Raul. The contract no longer stands.' She lifted her chin and glared at him, desperately trying to ignore the heat of his touch on her face.

'To hell with the contract.'

'How can you say that when the debt instigated such a deal with me? If I hadn't been able to find your brother, I dread to think how things would be now.'

'The passion and desire between us was inevitable, Lydia. As was the conclusion.'

How could he say that so soon after saying she was the woman he loved? It was all just words for him, words to get what he wanted, when money couldn't achieve that.

Before she could say anything his lips claimed hers in a hot, searing kiss that set light to every part of her body. Her limbs weakened and her lips softened as she kissed him back as if her life depended on it as he pulled her close. She loved this man, so why couldn't she believe him? So much had happened between them in the short time they'd known each other, but could a man who'd openly condemned love really love her?

She pushed against him, breaking the kiss with such force that he was forced to let her go and she stepped quickly back. 'My father's debts are settled, not by the funds for finding Max, but by those properties my father hid in my name. They are now yours, to do with as you please. You have everything you wanted, Raul, and I have lost just about everything. Just go.'

She turned from him, the sting of tears in her eyes, and she swallowed down the need to give into them. Raul's gentle touch on her arm was the last thing she'd expected after the dominating way he'd entered the shop and then claimed that kiss. She pinched the bridge of her nose, willing the tears to stay where they were.

'That's where you are wrong, Lydia. If I have lost you, I have lost everything.' Slowly he turned her to face him and she looked up at him, into eyes that no longer held the defensive glare. This was the real Raul, the man who, for whatever reason, feared love.

'I'm sorry, Raul, I can't love a man who doesn't know how to love, how to open his heart to the most natural emotion in the world.'

'Can you give such a man a chance?' The slight waver to the deep accented timbre of his voice told her so much. It also lit the small flame of hope within her.

'You told me love was not for you. How can things

have changed?' His touch on her arm seared her skin through her clothes and she longed to walk into his embrace, to accept love on his terms, but it wasn't enough.

'My mother knows we are in love.' He spoke softly, sending the conversation in a different direction and her mind into a spin of questions.

'That's because we acted the part—'

He cut her words off. 'She saw love beneath that, Lydia. My love for you and yours for me.'

She shook her head. 'No, that's not possible.'

'And Max. He saw it too.'

'You spoke of our deal to your brother?' She hadn't asked anything about that meeting, the humiliation of being sent from the room like a scolded child still very raw.

'He made it very clear I'd been too hard on you— and I was. He also told me I had much to settle with you and I'm guessing he knows that first hand, from the exchange I witnessed between him and his wife.'

'His wife? The lovely redhead waiting in the foyer?'

Raul nodded. 'And soon to be the mother of his child, but that is not important now. I have been a fool, Lydia, hiding from your love, trying to deny that I felt the same for you, seeing it as a weakness. But all that has changed.'

'It has?' The whisper her voice had become held so much hope that her heart ached.

'I've changed and it is because of you. I'd give up

all my wealth, my father's inheritance, everything if it meant I could have you in my life, as my wife. I love you, Lydia.'

'I don't need anything else but your love, Raul.' He stroked his fingers down her cheek as she spoke and she closed her eyes against the sensation. When she opened them his eyes were so full of love that she wondered how they could ever have been so cold and hard. 'I love you, Raul.'

This time the kiss was gentle and loving, leaving her in no doubt that his words were far more than that. They were real, as real as their love for one another. She trembled as he took her in his arms, holding her to him so that she could hear the beat of his heart. Right here was all she'd ever wanted.

'Just one more thing.' Raul's voice was filled with emotion as he spoke and moved her from him so he could look at her.

'What is it?' Lydia looked up at him to see a smile of love on his lips and she had to resist the urge to kiss him again.

'With all the upheaval of finding Max and then losing you, I haven't cancelled our wedding.'

'But that's just days away.' Was he suggesting they get married as planned on Christmas Eve in Madrid? If he was, she knew exactly what her answer would be. She didn't need a big fancy day.

'What do you think? Should we get married?' he teased her with soft words of Spanish.

'I can't think of anything better.' She smiled and then as his lips claimed hers allowed herself to slip into the bliss of his kiss, briefly at least. There was one more small matter to settle. 'There is one condition.'

'Which is?' His eyes narrowed in suspicion, but this time the smile on his lips proved he was teasing her.

'That Max and his wife are there too.'

'That would be the best way to begin married life, with my brother beside me to witness my love and commitment to you.'

EPILOGUE

SHE WAS MARRIED. Lydia looked at her husband as he talked with his brother and her heart filled with love for Raul. It was hard to believe that three days ago in London she had been in her boutique trying to piece together her life after Raul had sent her from his so sternly. Now they were man and wife. She was married to the man she loved, the man who loved her.

Raul turned and looked at her; the hotel room they'd hired for their small wedding party faded out of focus as he smiled at her. Not only did he love her, but that love was unguarded, bared for the few close friends and family members who'd witnessed their exchange of vows. The most important being his mother and brother.

Raul crossed the room to her. He looked stunningly sexy in his black tuxedo, the red band at his waist only adding to the overall effect and matching perfectly with her seasonal bouquet. She still couldn't believe she was married to him, the man of her dreams.

He swept her into an embrace and kissed her. A long lingering kiss full of the promise of so much more and, even though his mother was in the room, she responded. How could she not? He was everything she wanted and so much more.

'You look beautiful,' he said, barely moving away from her, his forehead almost against hers, his breath warm on her face.

'You approve, then?' she teased, recalling the panic she'd gone into trying to find the perfect wedding dress the weekend before Christmas. It had been a Spanish designer she'd met earlier in Madrid who had come to the rescue. The dress fitted as if it had been made for her and the fur-trimmed hooded cape finished the 'winter bride' look perfectly.

'Of your use of a Spanish designer who created a dress almost as beautiful as you? Yes, I approve, but of you, as my wife, I more than approve.' His teasing voice left her in no doubt of how much he approved and her heart sang with joy as he kissed her again.

'It's been a perfect day,' she said wistfully.

'Even though your family are not here?'

'My grandmother is too frail to travel now, but she will meet you as soon as we return from our honeymoon, and as for my parents...' she paused, the hurt of her mother's excuses for not attending still cut deep, but her father's blunt refusal was no more than she'd expected '...let's just say time will heal. My father will get over the loss of his properties and my mother has invited us to her home in the new year.'

'So you are happy?'

'Perfectly.'

'Then it is time we went,' he said softly, a wicked gleam in his eyes. 'We will stay at my apartment for a few days, then head to London for Max's sister's birthday party. After that we will fly to the Seychelles for our honeymoon.'

She smiled at him. 'Sounds wonderful.'

'It will be. We can spend time alone and celebrate the start of a new year with our own fireworks.' The spark of mischief danced in his eyes.

'You are incorrigible, Raul Valdez, but I love you so very much.'

'And I love you too, with all my heart.'

'Do you have any idea how much it means to hear those words from you?' she teased him, interspersing her words with light kisses.

'And do you have any idea that I will be saying them to you every day from now on?'

'I'll hold you to that.'

'And I intend to show you just how much too—as soon as we are alone.'

She took his hand and looked up into his eyes. 'Let's go now, then.'

His handsome face had the sexy devil-may-care look on it and her heart melted. She loved him so very much—and he loved her. The future was theirs and full of love and happiness.

* * * * *

COMING NEXT MONTH FROM

⟨H⟩ HARLEQUIN
Presents®

Available November 21, 2017

#3577 HIS QUEEN BY DESERT DECREE
Wedlocked!
by Lynne Graham
King Azrael fights the temptation of his captive Molly Carlisle's curves, especially when they're stranded overnight in the desert. To protect her reputation, Azrael declares them married, but his announcement is legally binding—Molly is now queen! And Azrael wants his wedding night...

#3578 A CHRISTMAS BRIDE FOR THE KING
Rulers of the Desert
by Abby Green
Sheikh Salim Al-Noury is determined not to rule—until a beautiful diplomat is hired to persuade him to reconsider. Working abroad is Charlotte McQuillan's perfect getaway from Christmas heartbreak. But Salim's rugged masculinity soon awakens Charlotte to unimaginable pleasures!

#3579 CAPTIVE FOR THE SHEIKH'S PLEASURE
Ruthless Royal Sheikhs
by Carol Marinelli
Sheikh Ilyas al-Razim won't let a waitress attempt to blackmail him—even if that means taking stunning Maggie Delaney as his hostage. Maggie convinces Ilyas of her innocence and is freed... yet now she's held captive by their smoldering desire!

#3580 CARRYING HIS SCANDALOUS HEIR
Mistress to Wife
by Julia James
Brooding Italian Cesare di Mondave stole Carla Charteris's innocence. When Cesare discovers her pregnancy, he must claim his heir. Cesare decides to use every seductive skill he has to convince Carla he wants her in the bedroom *and* at the altar!

HPCNM1117RA

#3581 CHRISTMAS AT THE TYCOON'S COMMAND
The Powerful Di Fiore Tycoons
by Jennifer Hayward
Chloe dreads working with Nico Di Fiore, the man who once coldly rejected her. *Nothing* will distract Nico from success, including his craving for Chloe. But now, with their connection undeniable, Nico is determined to take Chloe as his own!

#3582 LEGACY OF HIS REVENGE
by Cathy Williams
After Sophie Watts crashes into Matias Rivero's car, she must work off her debt as his chef! Seeking revenge against Sophie's father, who ruined his family, Matias plans to seduce the truth from her... But he doesn't expect nine-month consequences!

#3583 A NIGHT OF ROYAL CONSEQUENCES
One Night With Consequences
by Susan Stephens
Prince Luca wanted a convenient bride—until sweet Callie reveals the consequences of their one sinful night! Having just taken back her freedom, Callie refuses to wear his ring. So Luca must show her the pleasures of life in the royal bed!

#3584 INNOCENT IN THE BILLIONAIRE'S BED
by Clare Connelly
Rio Mastrangelo is determined to sell his father's island as fast as he can. Potential purchaser Tilly Morgan's luscious body fills him with hot desire. When a storm hits, trapping them together, there's nowhere to run from their raging hunger!

HPCNM1117RB

Get 2 Free Books,
Plus 2 Free Gifts—
just for trying the
Reader Service!

HPI7R2

*Reluctant sheikh Salim Al-Noury would rather abdicate
than taint the realm with his dark secrets. But one
exquisitely beautiful diplomat might tempt him otherwise!*

*Christmas means heartbreak to Charlotte, and this
overseas assignment offers the perfect getaway. But
Salim proves to be her most challenging client yet, and
his rugged masculinity awakens untouched Charlotte to
unimaginable pleasures!*

Read on for a sneak preview of
A CHRISTMAS BRIDE FOR THE KING
by *Abby Green*,
part of her **RULERS OF THE DESERT** series.

Charlotte looked Salim straight in the eye. "Life is so easy
for you, isn't it? No wonder you don't want to rule—it would
put a serious cramp in your lifestyle and a dent in your
empire. Have you ever had to think of anyone but yourself,
Salim? Have you ever had to consider the consequences of
your actions? People like you make me—"

"Enough." Salim punctuated the harshly spoken word
by taking her arms in his hands. He said it again. "Enough,
Charlotte. You've made your point."

She couldn't breathe after the way he'd just said her
name. Roughly. His hands were huge on her arms, and firm
but not painful. She knew she should say "Let me go," but
somehow the words wouldn't form in her mouth.

HPEXP1117

Salim's eyes were blazing down into hers and for a second she had the impression that she'd somehow…hurt him. But in the next instant any coherent thought fled, because he slammed his mouth down onto hers and all she was aware of was shocking heat, strength and a surge of need such as she'd never experienced before.

Salim couldn't recall when he'd felt angrier—people had thrown all sorts of insults at him for years. Women who'd expected more than he'd been prepared to give. Business adversaries he'd bested. His brother. His parents. But for some reason this buttoned-up slender woman, with her cool, judgmental attitude, was getting to him like no one else ever had.

The urge to kiss her had been born out of that anger and a need to stop her words, but also because he'd felt a hot throb of desire that had eluded him for so long he'd almost forgotten what it felt like.

Her mouth was soft and pliant under his, but on some dim level not clouded red with lust and anger, he knew it was shock—and, sure enough, after a couple of seconds, he felt her tense and her mouth tighten against his.

He knew he should draw back.

If he was another man, he might try to convince himself he'd only intended the kiss to be a display of power, but Salim had never drawn back from admitting his full failings. And he couldn't pull back—not if a thousand horses were tied to his body. Because he wanted her.

Don't miss
A CHRISTMAS BRIDE FOR THE KING
available December 2017 wherever
Harlequin Presents® books and ebooks are sold.

www.Harlequin.com